# MARRIED BY SUNDAY

SARAH READY

CROWN

# ALSO BY SARAH READY

**Stand Alone Romances:**

The Fall in Love Checklist

Hero Ever After

Josh and Gemma Make a Baby

**Soul Mates in Romeo Romance Series:**

Chasing Romeo

Love Not at First Sight

Romance by the Book

Love, Artifacts, and You

Married by Sunday

**Stand Alone Novella:**

Love Letters

Find these books and more by Sarah Ready at:

www.sarahready.com/romance-books

Sign up to receive bonus content, exclusive epilogues and more at:
www.sarahready.com/newsletter

**WHEN OPPOSITES CLASH...**

Nathaniel Barry is monochromatic, meticulous, and uptight. Izzy Harris is wild, unpredictable, and free-spirited. Nathaniel has a trendy apartment, a successful career, and a girlfriend he's about to propose to. Izzy has no home, no career, and nobody special to hold her down.

They're polar-opposites in every way.

So when they sit next to each other on the train to Romeo, New York they clash from the very start. Naturally, Nathaniel decides he wants nothing to do with Izzy. And Izzy...well, she has a different opinion.

No matter how much Nathaniel protests, Izzy knows it was fate that brought them together. Nathaniel's girlfriend just ran off to marry another man, and Izzy swears she'll help

Nathaniel win her back. They have three days to stop the ill-advised wedding. It should be easy. It should be simple. But when two polar opposites team-up to stop a wedding, there's only one guarantee – that nothing will go as planned.

# married by sunday

## SARAH READY

CROWN

W.W. CROWN BOOKS
An imprint of Swift & Lewis Publishing LLC
www.wwcrown.com



Copyright © 2021 by Sarah Ready
Published by W.W. Crown Books an Imprint of Swift & Lewis Publishing, LLC, Lowell, MI USA
Cover Illustration & Design: Elizabeth Turner Stokes
Interior Line Drawings: Sarah Ready


Library of Congress Control Number: 2021914217
ISBN: 978-1-954007-27-7 (eBook)
ISBN: 978-1-954007-28-4 (pbk)
ISBN: 978-1-954007-30-6 (hbk)
ISBN: 978-1-954007-29-1 (large print)

# married by sunday

# 1

Izzy

WHEN I PRAYED FOR THE UNIVERSE TO GIVE ME A SIGN, GIVE me some reason to keep going, I didn't know it'd answer me so quickly.

But, like my aunt used to say, "be very careful what you wish for Izzy." Or, "Izzy, why oh why, are you always begging for trouble?"

Which is sort of the same thing, isn't it?

My train ticket says seat 9A. Business Class.

Not because I have loads of extra cash to throw away, but because I made a mistake at the ticket counter and didn't realize I picked the wrong section.

Penn Station was busy and dirty and loud and I had a choice to make. I was either going to make a date with a fifth of vodka and a park bench, or I was going to take a train to Albany and then a bus to Romeo.

Dread and resignation curl in my stomach. Of course, dread wins by a mile. I've avoided Romeo for too long. I've never been a coward, but I've been a coward in this.

Hence my prayer.

It went like this. *Hey up there, it's me, Izzy. You know the one. I'm in bad trouble. I don't think I can keep going. I don't think...send me a sign please?*

Then I started to cry, but we'll just gloss over that bit.

I sat on the grubby Penn Station steps. Old gray gum was flattened on the stone step next to me, a cockroach crawled over a dirty slice of sausage pizza, and my stomach let out a long, hungry growl. The pizza looked good to me, cockroach or no. The vodka and park bench sounded good to me too, cold rainy weather or no.

So I cried a bit.

But then, I looked up and a sliver of sun came out from behind the clouds. It flickered down on my face. And I thought, well that's a sign, I suppose.

But it wasn't.

The sign is sitting in 9A, my seat. And he's the most serious, focused, hardest man I've ever seen.

I stand still in the narrow aisle while the train starts to pull away from the station. I grab the seat back next to me and rock with the swaying motion of the train car. The straps of my oversized backpack dig into my shoulders and an annoyed older man in a business suit elbows me as he shoves past.

I don't really notice.

Because, *this man.*

He's my sign. There's no doubt about it.

I'm not sure why he's my sign, why he's here, or why there's a little niggle inside me saying "you asked, Izzy, so here ya go," but I'm not about to tell the universe no thank you.

Somehow, I know, this man is going to help me.

**2**

———

Izzy

I clear my throat. "Excuse me." I hold my ticket out in front of me.

The man ignores me. He stares straight ahead at the back of the seat in front of him. He doesn't even look out the window at the brown brick facades, the graffiti or the gray apartment buildings whizzing by.

"Excuse me, sir. You're in my seat." I wave the ticket closer to his face. It's a nice face—thirtyish, dark, brooding.

He doesn't notice.

Another man with a giant briefcase tries to inch past me and my backpack. "Outta the way, love," he says in a gruff Brooklyn accent.

I squeeze against the seats, my thighs mash to the plastic

edge of the chair. The train hits a bump in the track and I grab the seat to keep my balance.

"Excuse me, mister. That's my seat," I try again.

Still nothing.

There are two seats. Maybe he's in 9B and wanted the window. But maybe not. I don't want to sit in 9B and then have the real ticket holder come along and kick me out. I shimmy into the row and lean close to the man, then I wave my ticket in front of his face.

"Sir?"

Finally, finally, he turns and looks at me.

My mouth goes dry.

"Don't do this," he says with desperate intensity.

"What?" I squeak.

"You don't know what you're saying. For crying out loud, you met him last night, you can't possibly—"

A hot blush spreads across my cheeks. He's on the phone.

Apparently, this isn't a happy conversation.

The train rounds a bend and I stumble a bit. I decide to take off my backpack and claim 9B. The man continues and I can't help but overhear.

"Don't do anything rash. No. Don't. No, I didn't..." He speaks in a low, intense voice. "You can't just throw away three years. We—"

I tuck my backpack under the seat in front of me then lean back. My stomach growls, pretty loud too, but the man doesn't notice. He turns away from me, toward the window.

I take a second to study him.

He's wearing an expensive, perfectly tailored, navy blue

suit and polished black shoes. His shirt is bright white and he has a red tie and a precisely folded pocket square.

I notice his watch is worth more money than I've had in a good while. His dark hair is just barely long enough to curl over his ears, a mere quarter inch of imperfection.

By the way he sits, stiff and at attention, and by the way he dresses, like his clothing was pressed with a hot iron and a ruler, and by the way he speaks with sharp articulation, I'd say that this man hasn't had a moment of fun in years. In fact, I'd bet the farm that he hasn't laughed in years.

Poor guy.

"You can't possibly love him. You can't fall in love with someone in twelve hours. Be reasonable," he says in a tone that says he's striving for logic.

I can't make out the words on other end of the conversation, but I do hear a high-pitched, impassioned reply.

I look up at the ceiling of the train and shake my head. Guaranteed he's not going to get through to her.

"Do not get married on Sunday," he says forcefully. "I'm coming. We'll talk. Don't do anything rash. Please. This is insane."

I agree with him, wanting to get married on Sunday never turns out well. Guests prefer Saturdays.

The woman on the other end of the line replies, but I'm distracted by the appearance of the snack cart. Mmmmm. Food. Glorious, glorious food.

A large-nosed man in a neat uniform stops at my seat. There are delicious, delicious smells coming from his cart.

"Beverage? Something to eat, ma'am? Sir?"

I sigh and glance at the man sitting next to me. He's ignoring the snack cart. Obviously.

My stomach lets out a long, pathetic growl. I haven't eaten in nearly two days, not since landing at JFK airport. And I spent the last of my money on this train ticket and the bus ticket after.

"Sir?" the snack cart man says. "Coffee?"

The man next to me gives the snack cart vendor a distracted look and then a sharp nod. He holds up his finger to indicate he'd like one large coffee.

Well. He's not very friendly, is he?

But he is getting coffee...

My stomach gives a tight hungry clench. I make my decision, because honestly, hunger is a great motivator. Plus, it's fate.

"Devon, anything else?" I ask.

I've decided that the man next to me is named Devon. He looks like a Devon.

Clearly, he doesn't answer, because he's on the phone, ignoring everyone but the crazy-in-love lady on the other end.

I turn back to the snack cart man and smile apologetically. "He's on the phone with his sister, she's causing him all sorts of trouble. You see, my husband and I are on our honeymoon and all we wanted was a little time to ourselves. But family..." I shrug. "You know how it is."

"What does he want then?" asks the man impatiently. There are gobs of people waiting for snacks in the rows ahead of us.

I tilt my head and study the menu pasted to the side of the cart. I lick my lips.

"He'll have that coffee with cream and sugar. A ham and cheese croissant. A chocolate chip muffin. And, hmmm a bag of salt and vinegar chips."

The snack vendor grunts and starts pulling out the food. I horde it, gathering it on my lap.

"Anything for you?"

I nod, my eyes going glassy from the food smells wafting up to me. "I'll have a blueberry muffin. An apple. Another ham and cheese croissant. And a large coffee, no cream, but lots of sugar."

My stomach twists again and I lick my lips.

I set the food in my lap, and then pull out the tray to put the coffee on. It's steaming and smells so good that I almost start crying again.

The vendor uses an old blocky calculator to ring up the total.

"Twenty-six dollars," he says.

I look at the vendor, then I look at Devon, then back at the vendor and shrug.

"Please. You can't possibly get married Sunday. Fine. Bye. I'll see you—" Devon sighs and clutches his head for a second then he turns to the vendor. It looks like his phone conversation is done. "How much?" he asks.

"Twenty-six dollars."

Devon's eyebrows scrunch down and he scowls at the vendor. "For a large? How much do you charge for a small?"

The large-nosed vendor rolls his eyes. "The coffees are

four dollars. The croissants ten. The muffins eight. The apple-"

"I don't want all that, I just want coffee."

"Your wife ordered for you," the vendor says.

"What wife? I don't have a wife." Devon looks a little confused and a whole lot offended.

I give the vendor a sweet smile. "It's a game we play. Being newlyweds. Devon thinks it's funny."

Devon gives me an appalled look, and I think he's only just realized that I'm in the seat next to him. "Excuse me? We're not married."

I look back at the vendor. "See?" I open my eyes wide and flutter my lashes. "Come on Devon, don't be that way."

I didn't think it was possible, but Devon becomes even more stiff-backed and starched looking.

The vendor sighs, clearly at the end of his patience. "Come on, Devon. Buy your wife the food. Twenty-six bucks."

"We're not married," he says, then something else dawns on him. "And my name's not Devon!"

I roll my eyes. I think the vendor's starting to get angry.

"I don't care what your name is. I just want you to pay for the food your wife ordered."

"She's not—"

An exceptionally tall man a few rows up from us stands up and shouts over the seat, "Hey, funny guy, pay for your wife's food so we can get our coffee."

"Exactly! Thank you!" an old battle-ax of a grandma adds.

Devon's cheeks turn bright red and I can see the war

taking place inside him. Make a scene and fight the injustice of the crazy lady next to him, or pay the bill and avoid the scene. I smile sweetly when he pulls out his leather wallet and stiffly counts out thirty dollars.

"Keep the change," he says, shoulders stiff.

"Thanks, Devon. Enjoy your honeymoon," says the vendor. He shoves his cart down the aisle to serve the next row of passengers.

I sit still, relishing the weight of the food in my lap. Yum. Food.

Devon lets out a low growl. He's mad. Really, really steaming mad. In fact, I can feel the heat rolling off him. His eyes are sort of like those laser beams that sear your skin.

I hold out one of the warm foil-wrapped croissants. The crinkly noise the foil makes has my heart doing a happy dance.

"It's ham and cheese. I hope you're not a vegetarian. Or a vegan, you're not a vegan, right? No, you wouldn't be, your shoes are leather."

I drop the croissant into his hand and say, "Enjoy!"

He gives me an incredulous look. "What's wrong with you?"

Lots. Lots and lots. But while I'm with Devon, I'm not going to think about it.

I take a big bite of my croissant. Oh holy heaven, the cheese is all melty and gooey and the croissant is so buttery. A soft little moan escapes.

His eyes flick to my mouth and I lick a crumb from my lips. So good. It's so good. Devon seems sort of stunned.

"Don't you like ham and cheese? I got you a chocolate

chip muffin too, or you can have my apple if you want? But really, you should try this croissant. It's like heaven in your mouth."

He shakes his head and stares at me with morbid fascination. "Are you insane?"

"Hmm?" I take another bite, yup, still amazingly delicious, and then I swallow some of the steaming coffee.

"Are you insane? Or a scam artist? What?"

I frown. "Devon, please. I didn't mean anything by—"

He throws up his hands. "For crying out loud, my name isn't Devon. It's Nathaniel. Nathaniel Barry."

I smile widely and hold out my free hand for him to shake. "Izzy Harris, I'm so pleased to meet you."

## 3

---

Izzy

"No." Nathaniel shakes his head vehemently and refuses to take my hand. "I don't want to meet you. Forget I told you my name. I wish I'd never introduced myself."

I drop my hand and set down my croissant on the seatback tray, "Oookay. I like Devon better anyway."

"Do you do this often? Accost perfect strangers minding their own business and scam them? Because you're really good at it."

I smile and start on the blueberry muffin.

"Thank you," I say between bites. The blueberries are tart and sweet at the same time, and there's a brown sugar crumble on top. I give another little moan.

He stares at me in shock. His eyebrows come together

and form a little wrinkle in the middle. It's the only wrinkle on him, so it stands out.

"Never mind," he says. "Don't speak to me again. Don't look at me. Don't do anything involving me. Got it?"

I frown. I'm not exactly sure why the universe thought I needed a super-grumpy, uptight sign, but maybe...maybe when he's helping me, I'll be helping him.

"Who were you talking to on the phone?" I ask.

He gives me another incredulous stare. He jabs his finger from me to him. "You and me, we're strangers. We don't talk. Okay?"

Huh.

Well, at least my stomach is happy. The blueberry muffin and croissant are gone, so I buff the apple and take a big bite. The crunch is overly loud in the tense silence.

Devon, aka Nathaniel, sighs then pulls out his phone and starts texting furiously.

Once my apple's gone, I take another swig of my coffee. Then, I realize that Nathaniel's coffee is still on my tray table. He never took it. Maybe a coffee would improve his mood.

I grab the paper cup, now lukewarm, and push it toward him. "You should try the coffee it's—"

The train hits another bend, and instead of kindly handing him the cup of coffee I throw it on him.

The cup tumbles through the air.

It smacks his chest, the plastic lid pops off, and sixteen ounces of milky, sugary, snack cart coffee drenches his white shirt, navy suit, red tie, and crisply folded pocket square.

My mouth drops open and a little squeak comes out. Everything freezes for just one second.

There's a stunned look on Nathaniel's face. Coffee drips down from his hard, stubble covered jawline to his neck. His pristine white shirt is now a see-through light brown. His cell phone lets out a little buzzing vibration and then the screen goes dark. Dead.

Oh.

Oops.

He lifts his furious eyes to mine and he lets out a low, angry growl.

Neither of us moves.

I think he's restraining himself, because it sort of looks like he's furious. Which I think is probably a new emotion for him. He was Mr. Calm, Cool and Collected before, all logic and reason with the lady on the phone, but now he's struggling to pull in a calming breath.

Oh boy. This is trouble. Exactly what Aunt Gerry always says, why oh why, do I have to go begging for trouble?

So, maybe he wasn't my sign, maybe I made that bit up because I was desperate for a little help. Because I'm scared. Because I don't know how to do this. But...ugh.

The train starts to slow down and I see that we're coming to a station. A voice on the loudspeaker declares that we'll be having a ten-minute station stop.

I lift my eyes and look at Nathaniel from below my lashes. He's still glaring at me, his jaw clenched, likely contemplating where to hide my body.

Outside on the station platform I see there's a little concession area, and hanging on the back wall are a few t-shirts.

I perk up. That's a solution.

"Come on. There are t-shirts out there. Let's go grab one real quick." I point at the little shop.

He looks out the window and scowls.

"It's really trendy to wear t-shirts under suit coats. Come on." I look down at my watch. We've got eight minutes. "Plus, they might have one of those cheap prepaid phones. Because...you know..." I gesture at his ruined cell phone. "You might want to call someone?"

Like the crazy-in-love lady.

He raises an eyebrow.

"I'm sorry," I say. "I didn't mean to spill the coffee, but I'm trying to make amends here."

I stand and wave my hands in a *hurry up* sort of gesture. He sighs and looks down at his sticky, ruined shirt.

"Fine." He stands. Coffee drips off of him and his shoes squelch.

I hurry down the narrow aisle toward the door and jump onto the platform. I left my backpack under the seat, but I don't think any of the business people are going to rifle through my dirty underwear and used paperbacks in the next few minutes.

Nathaniel steps down after me. He's taller than I thought. At least six foot two, nearly a foot taller than me. Yeah, I'm pixie short.

I hurry toward the metal concession stand. There's a woman inside bundled up in a puffy winter coat and a fuzzy hat. The damp autumn air does have a way of seeping into your bones and chilling you from the inside out.

"Excuse me," I say politely. "Do you happen to have

any..." I look over at Nathaniel and study his broad shoulders and tall frame. "Extra-large t-shirts?"

The woman frowns at Nathaniel's stained clothing. "No. There's a store downstairs," she says.

I look at my watch. We still have six minutes. "We've got time. Come on."

He looks back at the train. I can tell that he wants to play it safe, he seems that like that kind of guy, but then he shivers at a chilling gust of wind that presses his wet shirt against his skin. "Alright, let's go," he agrees.

He takes the stairs two at a time. The stairs are metal and clang as we hurry down. The air smells like it does right before the leaves begin to fall, earthy and cold, so that it tickles your nose. We come to the bottom of the steps and Nathaniel stops so suddenly that I almost run into his back.

"It's closed," he says.

Sure enough. The little tchotchke gift shop is gated shut and the lights are off. The rest of the lower level is just empty storefronts.

"Oh. Well, that's okay. We'll find something in Albany, or..."

I trail off at the look that crosses his face. It makes the hair on the back of my neck stand on end. He's not looking at me though, he's looking behind me.

"Why, hello there," a voice calls. I tense, because I recognize that voice. No, I don't know the person who spoke, but I recognize the intent.

We're about to be robbed.

**4**

---

Unfortunately, this isn't my first time. I was robbed once, late at night in Milan, Italy, in a deserted train station. Similar to this one actually. I was lucky, they just wanted my money.

Slowly, I turn around and take a step closer to Nathaniel.

He may be a stranger and not like me very much, but he's clearly the better option here. He's not happy. I can tell. His day seems to be going from bad to worse.

Three men loom at the top of the stairs.

I've traveled on my own long enough to know when to cross the street, and these three men would make me cross the street. It's not their appearance, it's the look in their eyes. Also, the tallest man in the center, the one with the shaved head who doesn't seem to have a neck, he has a gun tucked in his waistband.

I quickly glance at Nathaniel. He doesn't seem scared, he seems angry.

"Keep your head," I whisper. "Just give them what they want."

"Do you know them?" he asks incredulously. He looks down and gives me a furious stare.

"No! Are you kidding? Why would you think..." I trail off. I can see how it might look like I purposely made him show how much money he has in his wallet through my "food scam," then spilled coffee on him to lure him to meet my "buddies" at the deserted station.

His lip curls.

Then he looks around. I've already figured it out though. We're trapped. From what I can see, the lower level of the station is closed off. The closest exit door is barred. The only way to exit is back up the stairs to the platform. The group of men slowly descend the stairs. I keep my eyes on the no-neck bald one with the gun. He seems a little unhinged.

Unbelievable, Izzy. Give me a sign, I said. Give me a reason to keep going. I didn't exactly mean let me get robbed of my last few cents. But I guess beggars can't be choosers.

Plus, my aunt always claimed there isn't any situation I can't talk my way out of.

So...here goes.

"Hiya." I beam up at them, putting my smile on full wattage.

The man on the left, the one in the wife-beater—and honestly, who wears a wife beater when it's forty-five degrees out?—stumbles a bit when he sees my smile. Even in rumpled clothes that haven't been washed in a week and dirty hair, I still can stun them. Thank you, Mom, for the showgirl genetics.

"What are you doing?" hisses Nathaniel.

"Gettin' us outa this fix," I whisper out the side of my mouth.

"Are you crazy? Get behind me. It's not safe."

I ignore him.

"Get behind me," he commands more forcefully.

I ignore him again.

This situation needs delicacy. I decide to lay on the honey and thicken my southern drawl until it's pouring out of me like sweet peaches and sunshine.

"We're just catchin' the train, if y'all don't mind. We're on our honeymoon." I give another high-beam smile and reach over and grip Nathaniel's arm. He stiffens and starts to pull away.

"Play along," I whisper.

Nathaniel doesn't relax, but he also doesn't pull away.

"Is that right?" Says the no-neck one with the gun.

I nod and make doe eyes. "Sure enough," I say. But I make it sound like "sho nuff." "Just have to slip upstairs and catch the train so we can give our regards to my sweet gran. She's on her death bed and all she wants to do is bless us. She wants us to name the baby after her." I reach down and put my hand over my abdomen. The man on the right has an elaborate cross tattooed down his neck. I make my smile a little more demure. "She's a devout Catholic and she wants to give her blessing."

"Ain't that nice," says No-Neck. "Honeymooners."

He doesn't say it like it's nice though.

Nathaniel hasn't said anything, but beneath my hand his arm is as taut as a lion about to spring.

"Y'all remind me of my cousins," I say. "Gran would like you too. She makes the best peach pies." Oh jeez, what am I saying? I don't have a gran.

The man in the wife-beater finally comes out of his smile-induced stupor. "Where you from?" He has a southern accent too.

"Georgia," I say and I give him a big smile. "You sound like a Texan, am I right?"

He nods. "Yes, ma'am."

"People are so much nicer down south, aren't they?" Please, please be nice.

"Yes, ma'am."

I squeeze Nathaniel's arm and start to tip toe up the stairs. Oh lordy, please let this work. Please let them think twice about robbing or shooting the nice, sweet, honeymooning couple with the baby and the dying gran who makes blue ribbon peach pies.

We climb the steps, and I try to keep my limbs loose and relaxed, even though I want to tighten up and run screaming up the steps. Nathaniel is grim next to me. Hopefully they don't look at him.

"Alrigthy then. You pay your respects to your gran," Wife-beater says.

"We will," I promise.

Finally, we've almost slipped past them when No-Neck says the words I was dreading. "Hang on."

I don't want to stop, we're almost to freedom. In a few more steps we'll be up to the platform, to blue sky, and fresh air, and the train.

"Where's your wedding rings?" he asks.

I look down at our hands. Neither of us are wearing rings.

Nathaniel sighs and shakes his head. Of course, his reaction gives us away.

No-Neck pulls the gun out of his waistband. "That's what I thought," he says. "Let's do this nice and easy. Give me your wallets, your phones, your jewelry, that nice watch."

I reach down into my pockets.

"Slow," says No-Neck.

Nathaniel hasn't said anything to the men. In fact, if I didn't know that he could talk, I'd think he wasn't able to. I turn out my pockets—there's my train ticket, one dime, three pennies, and a stick of gum that I was saving for when I got reallllly hungry.

"Your earrings," No-Neck says.

I give an inward shrug. He'll learn soon enough that I bought them from a drugstore for ninety-nine cents. I hand everything over to Wife-beater.

"You ain't married?" he asks reproachfully. "What about the baby?"

I give him a hurt look. "'Course we're married. What, you think I'd live in sin? What would my gran say? She's having Father Brady bless our rings. It's her last wish."

There. Suck on that.

"Hand it over," No-Neck points his gun at Nathaniel.

Nathaniel pulls out his leather wallet and tosses it to Wife-beater. Then he tosses him his dead phone.

"Your watch too," the tattooed one says.

Nathaniel unclasps his watch and drops it in the man's hand.

On top of the platform, an announcement begins. Our train is about to depart.

My throat constricts and I try hard to pull air in. If we're left behind, if we're left on this platform with these three men...

"Well, thanks so much," I say. "We'll just be catching our train now."

No-Neck shakes his head. "Your shoes too."

I look down. I'm wearing a pair of ratty old Converse, so old the rubber is peeling off. "My shoes?"

"Not yours. His. Those are three-thousand-dollar shoes. The belt too."

I turn with wide eyes to stare as Nathaniel pulls off his shoes.

His jaw is tight and his movements are stiff. He sets the black leather dress shoes carefully on the steps in front of him. They clank against the metal. Then he yanks off his belt in a tight movement.

I see the moment that the men realize his belt could be a weapon because No-Neck cocks his gun and shakes his head. Nathaniel sets the belt on the ground next to his shoes.

The whooshing noise of our departing train fills the stairwell. It's loud chuffing is almost a desperate pleading— hurry up, hurry up, chuff chuff chuff.

"Okay," I say, "thank you. Have a good day now."

I grab Nathaniel's hand. We can run. We can run and make it before the train pulls out of the station.

The men move to block our path and my stomach drops down to the cold metal steps. I'm going to throw up. I just had the most delicious meal I've eaten in weeks and I'm going to throw it up less than an hour after enjoying it. This is karma, it must be a rule, anything eaten through deceit will be lost through puking.

"Your suit too. Pants and jacket."

"Excuse me?" Apparently taking off his clothes is the last straw for Nathaniel. His crisp enunciation has a huge helping of restrained fury.

"You heard him," Tattooed Cross says. And I'm sure, just sure, that Nathaniel's suit will bring them a nice pocketful of cash.

The sound of the train, the whooshing and the chuffing have disappeared. We've been left behind. I really am going to puke.

Maybe I should scream. Maybe I should've screamed in the first place.

Except, there's no one downstairs, no one in the ticket booth, and only the woman in her concession stand upstairs.

Nathaniel drops his jacket on top of his shoes. The suit is soft blue wool with satin lining. It's really lovely actually.

His long fingers pop open the button on his pants and then he pulls down the zipper. I've never heard such an angry unzipping. He steps out of his pants and drops them to the growing pile.

I put my hand on his arm again and try not to look at him. He's in tight black briefs, his coffee-stained dress shirt, the red tie, and black socks. His legs are long and muscular, dusted with dark hair the same shade as the blue-black hair on his head.

"May we go now?" he asks in his clipped voice.

No-Neck looks at me, and the skin on my neck starts to crawl. There are suggestions of things in his eyes that I don't want to consider.

"My gran's waiting," I say perkily. "On her deathbed," I remind them, "with Father Brady at her side."

The shutters in No-Neck eyes close. "Alright then."

Wife-beater bends down and scoops up the clothes and the shoes. "Congratulations on your wedding. And the baby."

My head feels woozy.

"Thank you," I say.

The men turn and run up the stairs. In seconds they're gone.

I start to shake. I'm still clutching Nathaniel's arm. After a long, silent moment he turns and looks at me.

"You," he says.

I swallow. "Me?"

"You."

That's all he says. After that he hurries up the stairs to try to find someone to report the robbery to. There's no one.

The woman's shop is closed. No one's on the platform. The map on the wall shows the nearest town, a tiny little burg, is six miles away.

I stand on the platform, my hands folded in front of me, biting my bottom lip nervously.

Nathaniel finally comes and stands next to me. The sun

is sinking beneath the horizon and there's a definite chill in the air. He must be freezing. Heck, I'm in a sweater and jeans and I'm freezing.

"There's no one here," he says.

I nod. "The map shows a town six miles down the road. We could walk. Maybe flag someone down. I could convince them to give us a ride, maybe get us to Albany—"

"Look," he cuts me off, "what's your name again?"

I raise my chin. "Izzy."

"Alright, Izzy. We aren't friends, we aren't even acquaintances. In fact, I wish I'd never met you. We had a very unfortunate experience together. You can walk to town with me. We won't talk. Not one word. Because we aren't friends. When we get to town, we'll go our separate ways. Okay?"

For once, I can't think of anything to say.

"Why do you look surprised?" he asks.

I clear my throat. "I guess, I thought you were nicer than this."

He raises an eyebrow. "What possibly could've given you that impression?"

I narrow my eyes.

Okay, he is my sign. He is definitely, one hundred percent, absolutely, without a doubt my sign. Nathaniel Barry needs a dose of fun, of nice, and of happy, and I'm going to give it to him.

And by helping him, I'll be helping me.

**5**

---

NATHANIEL

WHEN I WOKE UP THIS MORNING LIFE WAS NORMAL.

Life was good.

I read the *New York Times* with my coffee and egg white omelet. I worked out from five-thirty to six-thirty. I made it to the office by eight.

The courier from the jeweler brought the engagement ring at ten. At eleven, old Wisebrook, the senior partner at Wisebrook and Bleakerman, stopped by to hint that the partners would be discussing my promotion to their ranks at the annual meeting. Everything was perfect.

I was going to be promoted to partner and get engaged in the same week. Could life get any better?

No. No it could not. But apparently it could get a lot worse.

I bite back a curse when I step on a shard of glass from a broken beer bottle.

Izzy and I are at least a mile down the pothole-ridden country road heading toward the closest town. Not a single car has passed us since we left the train station.

The sun is gone, the cold is here, and bugs and birds are making noises in the scrubby trees lining the edge of the road.

"Are you okay?" Izzy asks.

"Fine," I bite out. I limp a bit until the stinging in my foot stops.

"Are you sure? I could look at it. You don't want it to get infected."

This is the first time Izzy's spoken since we left the train station. I didn't think she'd actually last a whole mile. She doesn't seem like the kind of person who's comfortable with quiet.

"Ya know, you seem kinda wound up," she says.

Her words lilt up and down, like the hills of some lush southern county. A man could lose his head listening to her.

Gravel crunches under my socks and I wince at another, sharper stabbing pain in my foot. I pause, yank off my sock and peer at the bottom of my heel in the gray light of dusk. There's some blood dripping out of a half-inch long slice, but I don't think any glass lodged in my foot.

Izzy comes close and leans down for a good look.

"Huh."

I expect her to say more, but she doesn't. I drop my foot and start walking again, ignoring the pain.

"So, who were you talking to on the phone?" Izzy asks.

She has to take two quick steps to keep up with one of mine.

I imagine most men would think she's stunning. She has that honey-blonde, doe-eyed, luscious-lipped, pin-up girl sort of quality that short circuits men's brains.

She even has a voice that sounds like music. But it only takes about two seconds in her company to realize that she's completely insane. I avoid crazy like the plague. I can't wait to get to town and part ways.

"Was it a friend?" she asks. "Or your sister? Oooh. Is your sister running off to marry the local bad boy? Does he have a motorcycle?"

I don't answer. I'm having trouble not thinking about the scene in the train station. My blood ran cold when I saw those men look at Izzy. I don't know if she realized their intent. I would have given anything to keep them from hurting her. I don't even know her, I don't really like her, but I don't want to see her hurt.

"So, is your sister in Albany?" she asks.

I frown. "I'm not going to Albany."

The trees nearby rattle as a cold wind whips through. I think the temperature has dropped to the low forties and here I am in a damp shirt, boxers, and silk socks. I pick up my pace.

"Where are you going then? Where's your sister getting married?"

"She's not my sister," I say in annoyance, thinking of the engagement ring at home on my dresser.

"Mmmhmm," Izzy says.

I can practically hear her teeth chattering. This road is

the epitome of country. It's chewed up gravel, ditches with tall weeds, a scrubby forest, and not a single house for the whole time we've been walking.

"I'd give you my shirt, but it's still wet. It'd probably make you colder," I say.

Izzy looks at me in surprise. "Hey now, I thought you weren't nice."

I frown at her, "I'm not. Your shivering is annoying."

"Uh huh," she says. "So where you headed to? I might be able to hitch us a ride together. I once hitchhiked five hundred miles."

I'll bet she did.

"Romeo," I finally admit.

"Really?" Izzy says. She sounds delighted. "That's where I'm heading! What're the chances of that?"

**6**

---

Nathaniel

A screech owl lets out a loud shriek, and I think it probably feels the same way I do.

"Is somebody you know getting married there?" Izzy asks.

My shoulders stiffen and I try to unclench my jaw. "No."

"Really? I thought you said something about a wedding on Sunday. Between you and me, Sundays are a terrible day for a wedding."

We start to climb up a steep hill. The road is at a forty degree incline. Luckily the extra work seems to warm Izzy up. Overhead, the first of the early stars start to appear in the sky.

"How long were you with her?" she asks.

"Who?" I can't keep up with her conversational gymnastics.

"The woman who's getting married Sunday. The one who left you."

I give her a sharp look. For someone who plays dumb, she certainly is perceptive. Finally I admit, "Three years."

She considers this and then nods. We make it to the top of the hill. I can make out the lights of a very small town a few miles away. The town is only a dozen or so buildings, and it's surrounded by dark farmer's fields that look like the smudges of charcoal pencil across paper.

Izzy sets her hand on my arm but doesn't say anything.

It feels the same as when she set her hand on my arm while we were being robbed. I think she does it when she wants to comfort me. Funny that.

We start down the hill. I grit my teeth and try not to limp, or acknowledge the fact that I'm walking down a lonely road at night, in god knows where Upstate New York, in my underwear, with a stranger.

"Do you love her?" Izzy asks.

"We've been together three years," I say sharply.

"So?" She looks at me swiftly and then swipes her bangs out of her eyes.

"I was going to propose to her this weekend."

"And?"

"And what?" I stop walking and look down at her.

"None of that answers my question."

I don't understand this woman.

"Of course I love her," I say. It's an automatic response.

Izzy lifts her eyebrow and I realize I didn't sound convincing. "I love her," I say, with all the conviction I feel.

"And she's run off to Romeo to get married?" Izzy shivers. I look at her. I can't tell in the dark, but her lips look like they're tinged blue. I pull my tie loose and unbutton my shirt.

"Here. It's dry now," I hand my dress shirt to her.

Her eyes go wide as she takes in my white t-shirt and boxers. It's freezing out, but I bet I'm still warmer than she is. There's no weight on her to keep her warm.

"Take it," I say in a no-nonsense kind of way.

She smiles and then wraps my shirt over her sweater. "Thank you. Don't worry, I won't think you're nice."

"Good," I say gruffly.

Izzy looks thoughtful. After a minute she says, "What's her name?"

It takes me a moment to realize who she's asking about. "Gertrude's?"

"No. Uh uh." She shakes her head vehemently.

"What?"

"You don't love her."

*What?*

"Excuse me? I just told you I did."

She gives me a skeptical look. "Puh-lease. Have you had sex?"

I stop walking and give her a hard stare.

She puts her hands on her hips like a teacher giving a lecture. "You can't possibly enjoy sex with a woman named Gertrude."

"Excuse me? How do you know?" I start to stalk away from her down the road, but she hurries to catch up.

"It's impossible. What do you yell out? 'Gertrude, oh Gertrude, take me deeper, oh Gertrude, you ignite me, you make me so hot, you're so yummy, Gertrude, yes, Gertrude yes'...no. Doesn't work. Sorry."

I scowl at her ridiculous recitation. "You have no clue what you're talking about. Sex isn't an issue."

She gives a delicate little snort. I can't make out her expression but I can tell she's disbelieving.

"I'm gonna be cruel to be kind, Nathaniel. Gertrude's gone. She's been wooed by some stallion. She's starry-eyed, head over heels in love with another man. The sooner you accept it, the better. You should move on."

Unbelievable.

"She met him less than a day ago," I say through gritted teeth. "She can't possibly be in love. It's a momentary lapse of judgment. As soon as she sees me, she'll realize her mistake and come home. With me."

"Oookay," Izzy says, completely unconvinced. "What does the stallion do?"

I narrow my eyes. "I don't know."

"What's his name?"

That I do know.

"Raphael," I growl.

She snorts. "You're screwed."

I don't like how confident she sounds. "What's that supposed to mean?"

"Do you know how a man named Raphael makes love?" she asks, her voice liquid and smoky.

"Certainly not," I say, realizing as I do that I sound stiff and pompous.

"Well, I do. I've met plenty of Raphaels. Metaphorically. You're toast, buddy. You can't compete."

"I have no idea what you're talking about. I'll have you know, I'm about to be made partner, I have an MBA from—"

"La-di-da. Super boring, blah blah blah. Doesn't matter." She pulls on my arm to stop me from walking and then tugs me around. "Let me show you. I'll be Raphael. You be Gertrude."

"Are you kidding me?"

"Humor me," she says.

"Fine." I cross my arms over my chest and wait for Izzy to work her *Raphael magic*.

I'm not expecting anything drastic, so it stuns me when suddenly, she changes. One second she's mischievous and sprite-like, the next she's a smoky-eyed sex goddess.

She drags her pointer finger down my arm and looks up at me from beneath dark, feathery eyelashes.

There's a soulful depth to her eyes. Her skin glows in the evening light. Her lips part, just a fraction and the pink tip of her tongue darts out. I focus on her lips. Her cool fingers trail down my arm and then stop at the pulse point of my wrist.

What the...

"Where have you been? I prayed for you. I've been waiting for you," she says in a broken whisper.

For some reason, my chest feels tight and my head feels muddled.

"You...you have?" I've lost track of the conversation.

I swear there's a tear glistening at the corner of her eye. I want to reach up and wipe it away.

"I didn't think I could go on until I met you," she whispers.

Then she sets her other hand on my chest, right on top of my heart. The look she gives me, the heat coming from her hand, and the air between us, thick and full of promise, I want...I want to lean down and kiss her.

"Nathaniel," she breathes my name, there's a hitch in her voice and suddenly I'm picturing rumpled bedsheets and tangled limbs.

"Izzy?"

"Hmmm?" She looks up at me, her lips soft and welcoming.

Holy...

Suddenly, she shakes her head and her features snap back to mischievous imp.

She steps away from me and says with a saucy smile, "And that is how a Raphael makes love."

It takes about half a second for me to realize that I fell fast and hard for her "demonstration." Me, a man who is in love and wants to get married.

Who *is* this woman?

"Face it, Nate. You don't have a chance."

She winks then starts to walk toward town. Her hips sway sassily. I hurry after her.

"Don't call me Nate."

Without missing a beat she asks, "Can I call you Devon?"

"No." I frown at her.

"Uh huh."

"Do you really think that's all it took?" I ask. I'm off-kilter from her demonstration.

Izzy shrugs but doesn't look at me. "What does Gertrude do?"

"She's an accountant."

I think I hear Izzy mutter "*of course,*" but I can't be sure.

"Yup, I think that's all it took. A night of wild, amazing, uninhibited sex and romance. You never know, maybe he's her soul mate."

I scoff. "Yeah right."

"What? You certainly aren't."

"How do you know?" I don't give her a chance to answer. She doesn't know a thing.

I take quick, angry strides down the pavement. The sooner we get to this town, the better.

"You know what. You're out of your mind. My life went from bad to nightmare as soon as you entered the picture. You are the worst thing that could've happened to me. I could've been to Gertrude by now if not for you. We could've been on our way home. All this behind us. And you...you could've been doing...whatever it is you do. Harassing strangers. Depriving kittens of their mothers. Stealing food."

"Hey! A girl's gotta eat—"

"As enlightening as your opinions are, I don't agree with you. My life was fine. My relationship was fine. And as soon as I get to Romeo, I'm going to find Gertrude and we're going to go home. And you...I'll be happy if I never see you again. Because you are nothing but trouble."

"Uh huh," she says.

I throw up my hands and pick up the pace. There's only a

half-mile to the edge of town. I think I see a farmhouse. Thank goodness. I'll ask to use their phone.

Izzy jogs to catch up. "Do you still want to ride with me to Albany? I'm sure I can find a lift."

Wow. She doesn't know when to quit.

"As kind as the offer is, I don't need your help, not now, not ever..." I trail off, because standing on the rise in front of us is a big man wearing coveralls and rubber boots. He raises a hunting rifle and points it at my chest.

"Son, you better have a good reason for running around in yer skivvies. You're upsetting the missus and I don't take kindly to that."

Izzy smirks at me and I can only imagine she's thinking about how much I'd like her help right about now.

**7**

———

Nathaniel

I come into the living room dressed in an old pair of farmer Tom's jeans and a thick flannel shirt that's been patched a few times.

The jeans are light blue, about three inches too short and loose at the waist, the cuffs are frayed and the back pocket is stitched with white thread. I washed my foot in the bathroom sink and put on an old pair of Tom's leather boots.

When Izzy sees me, her eyes widen and then spark with humor. Her lips twist and I get the feeling she's laughing on the inside.

Not like she's laughing at me, but like she's inviting me to laugh with her. I raise an eyebrow and give her a *serious* look. She covers her mouth to hold back a snort.

When she does Tom and his wife Linda realize that I'm standing in the hallway.

"There he is," Tom says in his booming, friendly way.

They're seated on an old brown couch with half a dozen multicolored crocheted afghans. Izzy is on the love seat across from them, a lime green and purple afghan spread over her lap.

"Izzy was telling us about what happened," Linda says. She has gray and brown curly hair and is wearing a rainbow-colored crocheted shawl over a long denim dress. "Horrible. Horrible thing. You poor dears."

I nod in agreement and sink to the loveseat next to Izzy.

It's a tight fit and the cushions are so soft that we slide into the center until our thighs press together. I try to scoot away, but it's no use, we just keep falling back together.

Izzy clears her throat and I attempt to ignore the heat of her leg and the softness of her hip.

"Again, thank you for the clothing. I really appreciate it," I say.

"Don't think about it," booms Tom.

He has the ruddy, windburned complexion of someone who has spent years working outdoors.

They've been uncommonly kind after Izzy explained to Tom that we'd been mugged at the train station. Linda clucked over Izzy and forced tea and cookies on her while I used their landline to call my credit card companies and my bank to report the theft of my wallet. I also called the Albany train station and asked if they'd located the bags from seats 9A and 9B. They had.

Izzy turns her head toward the kitchen and subtly starts to sniff.

It's the warm fragrance of pot roast with roasted potatoes and carrots, browned butter and thyme. I haven't smelled that since I visited my grandmother when I was eight or nine.

It's exactly the sort of smell that I would imagine in a white painted farmhouse with comfortable furniture, wood paneled walls, too many afghans, and a china hutch with a collection of porcelain bells in the corner.

"If you don't mind my asking," I begin, "is there any way I can get to Albany tonight?" The sooner I get to Romeo the better. I told Gertrude I'd be there by seven, and looking at the cuckoo clock on the wall, I'm thirty minutes late.

Linda looks at me as if I've grown two heads. "From Clarksburg? Goodness no. The next train comes through tomorrow afternoon."

"That's...unfortunate," I say, which is a massive understatement.

Izzy bounces on the couch a bit. It's like she's incapable of sitting still. "We don't have any money for train tickets or a taxi anyway. We might just have to walk. How many miles is it?"

Tom scratches his beard and considers for a moment, "about seventy if you walk along the highway."

Linda swats at him, "Oh you old coot, don't tease them." She turns back to me, "Tom's going to Albany in the morning. You can ride with him."

"Truly?" says Izzy. She sounds absolutely delighted. "It's so lucky you found us." She looks over at me and gives a saucy grin. But then she deflates, "I forgot. We don't have anywhere to stay 'til morning."

"Pish posh," Linda says. "You'll stay right here. There's a guest room upstairs. We'll have dinner and then get you all settled in."

"Oh that's too much," begins Izzy. I want to elbow her. Where else are we going to sleep? The woods? In a ditch?

"Think nothing of it," Tom says. "Only thing..." He rubs his chin and considers us. "We're an upright, moral couple and we wouldn't feel right your sharing a bed under our roof if you aren't married. You did say you're married, right? The muggers stole your wedding rings?"

"Horrible, just horrible," Linda says.

Then they both stare at us and wait for us to confirm our marital status.

Unfortunately, my words to Izzy from before must have made an impression because she doesn't immediately jump in with a story about weddings and honeymoons and ailing grans.

Nope.

She merely turns to me and lifts an eyebrow.

My word. She's not going to say anything. She's waiting for me to confirm or deny.

I freeze in place. On the one hand there's a pot roast and a warm bed, on the other a cold night outside and no dinner. There's no choice really.

So even though it feels like I'm making a deal with the devil, I look into Izzy's dark blue eyes, and I say in a serious voice, "Of course we're married. In fact, we're on our honeymoon."

Izzy's eyes crinkle at the corners and she holds back a smile. I can feel the laughter vibrating off of her. I've done it, I've passed over to the dark side. All for a pot roast and a warm bed.

I raise my eyebrows and wait for her to acquiesce.

She gives a subtle shake of her head, like she can't believe me, then still looking into my eyes, she says, "Hard to believe, isn't it? We're newlyweds. Nathaniel and Izzy Barry."

She turns to Tom and Linda and beams at them. "We just love being married. Man and wife. Husband and woman. Entwined by our holy matrimonial vows."

I hold back a snort. She's laying it on thick.

"Well, congratulations! Congratulations! Good man," booms Tom. He jumps up from the couch and pumps my hand. Linda comes over and gives us both a hug that smells like woolly sweaters and floral perfume.

"Let's have dinner then. A congratulatory dinner. There's a Dutch apple pie in the freezer too," Linda says.

I think I hear Izzy give a little moan of delight but I can't be sure.

I don't know much about Izzy but there are a few things I can be certain of.

One, she's trouble, two, she loves food, and three, I feel sorry for the man that ends up with her, because, like I said, she's trouble.

## 8



I BUILD A SMALL MOUNTAIN OF PILLOWS AND ROLLED UP afghans in the middle of the queen-size bed.

I would've slept on the floor, but the guestroom is so small there isn't any floorspace. The room is just a bed with a brass frame, a purple quilt, a pile of lacy pillows and four walls less than a foot from the bed on all sides.

Somehow Linda did manage to fit a child-sized rocking chair with a dozen miniature teddy bears next to the foot of the bed, but that's it for decorations. These old farmhouses had some small bedrooms.

I slap the last of the pillows down and study the bed. It should be fine.

"What's this? The Great Wall of China? The Berlin Wall?

No, wait...Hadrian's Wall?" Izzy lifts an eyebrow, "don't most walls crumble? Or fall?"

I give her a flat stare.

"Are you worried I'm going to get handsy in the middle of the night?" she asks. Her eyes sparkle like this is a really amusing thought. "Shame on you, Nathaniel. I'd never dream of it."

I shake my head, "I'm just trying to be..." I search for an appropriate word but I can't find one, so I settle for, "...decent."

Izzy looks like she's holding back her laughter.

She's showered off and squeaky clean. Her face is a healthy pink and her hair is piled on top of her head. She's zippered up in one of Linda's floor-length flannel night gowns. Instead of looking ridiculous and matronly, like she should, she looks wanton.

I think it's the zipper.

A zipper down the front of an article of clothing, even an oversized nightgown, would make any woman look wanton. Which is why Gertrude would never be caught in a front-zipping dress or nightgown. Gertrude cares about propriety.

At least, she did.

Thinking of Gertrude makes me stack another lacy purple pillow on the barricade.

"You should relax more. Have a bit of fun in life." Izzy jumps onto the bed and starts bouncing. The frame creaks with her movement, it sounds suspiciously like another bouncing activity.

"Stop that," I hiss.

"Why?" Izzy keeps bouncing, and her cheeks flush. "Don't you like bouncing on beds?"

I glare at her.

"Not since I was a child," I say stiffly, trying to make a point.

It flies over her head. The groaning of the bed springs continues.

It sounds like we're having a vigorous round of post-dinner sex. Linda and Tom's bedroom is just across the hall. There's no doubt in my mind they can hear the groaning of the bed frame.

Finally, Izzy falls back onto the mattress. Her arms and legs splay out and her hair falls around her face. She tilts her head to look at me.

"Coming to bed?" she asks.

When I hesitate she says, "I promise I'll keep my hands to myself. Your virginity is safe with me."

"I'm not a—" I cut off my retort when I see the amusement in her eyes. "Fine."

I flick off the light and climb into the other side of the bed. The mattress groans and squeaks under me while I shift around trying to get comfortable.

I'm acutely aware that Izzy is lying on top of the quilt on the other side of the mound of pillows.

I can hear her soft breath and long sighs.

I can feel when she shifts and tugs loose an afghan to fold over herself.

I can smell the peach conditioner she used in the shower.

But even when I can't hear, or feel, or smell her I'm still

aware of her. It's a prickly, uncomfortable awareness. It's similar to the feeling you have when your foot falls asleep, the heavy numbness followed by blistering pins and needles. I want to shake the feeling away so I don't have to be uncomfortable anymore.

"I can't sleep," Izzy whispers.

I turn on my side and face the pile of pillows. "It's been thirty seconds."

"Still. I can't sleep."

"You could try closing your eyes and not talking."

"What do you and Gertrude do to fall asleep? The hanky panky?"

I sigh and cross my arms behind my head. "We don't sleep together."

The bed shakes as she shifts to peer over the pillows. "I thought you said sex wasn't an issue!"

I feel my cheeks heat. "It isn't. We have separate apartments. We don't share a bed."

"Oh. That makes sense."

The pins and needles discomfort grows. "What makes sense?"

The bed groans as she positions herself on the pillows and looks over them at me. I can barely make her out in the dark room. She's a light slash of skin and a soft cloud of long hair.

"It fits," she says.

I stare at the ceiling. "I don't know what you're talking about."

"You're in finance, right?"

I turn sharply toward her. "How'd you know that?"

She scoffs. "You finance guys are all the same."

I take a second to ponder that. "What else?"

"Look, I don't want you to get upset." She says this like she's doing me a favor by not elaborating.

"I won't get upset."

"Oookay." Then she leans back on the pillows and starts. "Let me know how I'm doing as I go."

"Alright." I sit up, prop my pillow on the brass frame and lean back.

"You and Gertrude were introduced through a mutual acquaintance."

"Sure," I say. That's not unusual, lots of couples meet that way.

"You had three pseudo-platonic dinner dates at white tablecloth restaurants where you discussed work and your life goals. After the third date you had your first kiss. Lips, but no tongue."

"After two dates," I say, somewhat irritated that she has everything else right.

"Alrighty. After that, you went exclusive, and dated for six months, with gradually increasing levels of intimacy. After six months she said 'I love you' and you reciprocated by saying 'I love you, too'. Mainly you said it because if you don't say I love you after six months, you may as well break up."

The spot between my shoulder blades has a weird little itch. "It's a common way to proceed in relationships. Dating, then love. Most of the population does it that way."

She continues. "After the 'I love you' came sex. Which was a perk. Except, not really. Because you've always wanted to make love in a boat, or in the woods, or in a changing room, but Gertrude isn't into that sort of thing like you are."

"I'm not into—" I begin to argue, but Izzy cuts me off.

"As your relationship continued, you discussed things like the tax benefits of marriage, whether you should continue to rent or own, where you would go on vacation if you could ever let yourself take one, where you saw your careers in five years, how many children are optimal, and so on and so forth."

"Every serious couple discusses these things," I say. "You're like a bad newspaper astrology section. Just put out generalized garbage and everyone will think you're talking about them."

I think I have a good point but she ignores me.

"So, after three years of enduring a comfortable dating life full of routine and boredom, you decide to pop the question. You have everything mapped out. Date for three years, check. Engagement for one year, check. Married for three years, then have the first kid. Another two years, then have the second kid. Unfortunately, your plans trap you so tight that there's no room to deviate and there's no room to live. You're always putting everything off until you've even put off living." Izzy pauses to take a shallow breath, then she says, "You forget how to live. And so you miss out on life. On everything."

I roll my shoulders and try to dislodge the heaviness that settled on me as she spoke. I stare at the oval outline of her face. Her dark blue eyes are unreadable in the blackness of the room.

Finally she asks, "How'd I do?"

"Well." I clear my throat. "Cinque Terre."

She shakes her head and the bed shakes with her movement. "What?"

I trace my hand over the stitching on the quilt. "I haven't had a vacation in nearly a decade." Making partner has precluded vacations. "If I ever let myself take one, I'd go to Cinque Terre."

I can't see her, but I can feel her smiling. The air always buzzes around her with a sparkling energy when she smiles.

"Really?" she asks. "Cinque Terre? Not Romeo? Because, it's Thursday, and tomorrow's Friday, so by my reasoning that means you're finally taking a vacation."

A slow smile spreads across my face, but I'm glad she can't see it. No reason to encourage her. Then I turn serious. "Rescuing my fiancée from Raphael isn't a vacation."

"Semantics," she drawls.

I shake my head. "Anyway, your conjectures on my love life are way off."

Well, at least ten percent off.

She lets out a short huff and then rolls off the pillows to sprawl on her side of the bed. "I figured," she says, not at all perturbed that I claimed her theories on my relationship were bogus.

I do wonder how she came up with all of that, especially for how specific she was.

"You're going to Romeo too?" I ask.

"Mhmm. That's what I said."

I narrow my eyes. "Are you meeting your boyfriend there?"

When I ask this, Izzy goes completely still and I get the

impression that for a moment she's holding her breath. Then she moves again and lets out another huff. "Why would you ask that?"

A little alarm bell goes off that tells me I hit the bullseye.

"Isn't that why people go to Romeo? For love?"

"Something like that," she says. Her voice sounds muffled by the dark.

"So what's he like?" I wonder at the kind of man who would date a whirlwind like Izzy.

"Who?"

"Your boyfriend, or fiancé, or whoever he is."

"Who said I'm meeting my boyfriend?" she asks, and for once she doesn't sound excited or thrilled to talk. She actually sounds dampened, or sad, or, if I hadn't seen her in action the past twelve hours, I'd say...depressed. But I'd bet the bank that Izzy never gets depressed about anything.

"Sorry," I apologize. "I had the wrong impression."

She's quiet for a moment, then she says, "No. You're right. I'm going to see him."

Her voice has a hollow, apprehensive note that makes my chest squeeze. What kind of man makes a vibrant, spontaneous woman so hesitant?

"If you don't want to see him, you shouldn't."

"I know," she says noncommittally.

It makes me angry. How can she give out advice so freely, yet not take any herself. "Is your relationship serious?" I don't know why I ask this question, but I find myself leaning forward to hear her answer.

Her voice is muffled by the pillows. "It was. We were going to get married."

Ah. I see now. She's a free spirit. She isn't the type to get married and settle down. "He doesn't want to let you go?" I surmise.

She makes a surprised noise in her throat. "No, he did. More like I can't let him go."

Oh. So we're more alike than I thought. She doesn't want to let her fiancé go, and I won't let mine go.

The bed rocks as she takes a moment to climb under the quilt. When the squeaking stops and the rocking settles, I say, "You should take your own advice."

After a moment she says, "What's that?"

I try to recall her exact words from our walk to the farmhouse. Maybe she needs to hear them too. "I'm gonna be cruel to be kind, Izzy. Your fiancé's gone. The sooner you accept it, the better. You should move on."

I wait for her to respond, but she doesn't. I haven't seen her stay quiet for more than a few minutes, but a good five minutes ticks by without either of us speaking. Izzy's breathing evens out and I think she's fallen asleep.

But the five minutes of silence gives me enough time to feel guilty about what I said. It's not actually true, is it? Neither of us needs to move on.

"Izzy?"

I wait until she shifts under the quilt and says sleepily, "Hmmm?"

"Never mind. I'm sorry I said that. Neither of us needs to move on. I'll get Gertrude back and you'll get...what's his name?"

"David."

"I'll marry Gertrude and you'll get your David back.

Maybe you and David will get married too. Nobody has to move on. How's that sound?"

She lets out a soft snort. "It sounds delusional, kinda frightening, and against the natural order of things."

I smile up at the ceiling. There's the sassy Izzy I've come to know. Her and her theories about my love life.

"You'll see, it'll all work out. Tomorrow we'll be in Romeo, everything will turn out perfect and we can go our separate merry ways. Back to our happy lives."

"Uh huh."

My smile turns into a grin. "Go to sleep. And remember your promise. No getting handsy."

I hear rustling and then a lacy pillow smacks me in the head. I let out an *oof* then pull the pillow off my face.

"Handsy that," she says, and I can tell she's feeling better.

I smother a laugh and tuck the pillow under my head.

"Night," I say.

"Oh, be quiet. I'm trying to sleep."

I close my eyes and breathe in the scent of peach conditioner. I try to think of Gertrude, of what I'll say, what I'll do when I get to Romeo, but instead my mind keeps drifting to images of sex in a boat, sex in the woods, sex in a changing room, sex in, of all places, Cinque Terre, with, of all people, Izzy.

I fall asleep, uncomfortable.

## 9

Izzy

Nathaniel and I wave goodbye to farmer Tom as he drives away.

Well, I wave. Nathaniel holds up his hand and looks serious and stoic.

I think pretending to be a happy newlywed for our oatmeal and sausage breakfast, and then for the hour-plus car ride with Tom wore him out. He didn't say much this morning, but I think he's worried about seeing Gertrude.

I know the feeling. Even with a hot, filling breakfast, my stomach has an empty gnawing pain. Romeo isn't far.

So, we made it to Albany.

It's not quite seven in the morning. The sun is just peeking over the horizon, spilling soft morning light over the red brick train station. There are a ton of morning commuters hurrying to catch the train south. The sunlight glistens on the huge windows and the tall glass tower that looks like a lighthouse.

I drop my hand when Tom pulls out of the parking lot and turn to Nathaniel.

"So. We made it," I say.

I give him a bright smile. He's still wearing the too-short jeans and old flannel that Tom gave him. Last night it made him look more approachable, even though he still hadn't really smiled or laughed, but today, even in his farmer outfit, he looks aloof.

In fact, he may as well be back in his Wall Street finance suit. He's serious and distant, just like he was when I first sat down next to him on the train.

I pick up my backpack and clutch it to my chest. "Thanks for calling about this."

I didn't let on yesterday, but I was real scared that it was lost. As soon as Nathaniel picked it up from the lost and found, I opened up the hidden compartment at the bottom of the side pouch and breathed a sigh of relief to find my old cell phone, my now expired bus ticket, my ID, and my bank card.

Granted, the bank card has twenty-two cents on it, but still. I don't know what I would've done if my phone was lost for good.

Nathaniel gives one short nod. "I had to get my briefcase. Don't go thinking I did it because I'm nice."

He doesn't smile, in fact, he looks completely serious, but there's a tiny lifting of his lips and a crinkle at the edge of his eyes. Huh.

I beam at him. He lifts an eyebrow.

"So, we made it," I say again.

"So you said," he says with a hint of humor in his voice.

I keep grinning at him. I'm on to him. He may be all buttoned up, but really, somewhere deep inside he wants to have fun. "I was thinking. We still have to get to Romeo. If you don't have any money on you, I could hitch us another ride. Maybe a trucker is heading that way. It'd be fun. Or I could finagle us some bus tickets. I once sang the whole of *Cats* on a street corner to get enough money for—"

"Izzy."

I stop talking.

His black hair glistens in the sunlight and I can make out little strands of dark brown and auburn. He didn't shave this morning and his jaw has a dark shading of stubble. He shakes his head no.

For some reason, my stomach drops.

"I have a friend here. I called him when I grabbed our bags. He's giving me a lift to Romeo. In fact, he'll be here in a few minutes."

My stomach soars back up, because, well, Nathaniel found us a ride, but then I realize he said *me* not us.

"Well, that's great," I say enthusiastically. "That's good. Real good. Real, real...good." I bite my lip.

Nathaniel gives me a considering look. "You have a way to get to Romeo, don't you? You have money in your pack? A bus ticket or someone to call?"

I know he saw me clutching my phone to my chest, and

checking my bank card earlier. I wasn't subtle about my relief.

I study Nathaniel's expression. He'd help me, I think, if I told him I have no money and no one to call. I'm sure he would. But...

He clears his throat, "Izzy, if you—"

"'Course I do."

I lift my chin and give him a brazen smile.

"I've still got my bus ticket. I was only worried about you. Figured you were penniless, all alone in the world, and needed help getting to your Gertrude."

He shakes his head, and he's about to say something more, but then a dark blue Mercedes pulls up and the driver, a middle-aged man with stubbly gray hair gives a sharp wave.

"That your ride?" I ask.

Nathaniel looks over at the Mercedes then nods. "That's him. A work colleague."

The man waves again and Nathaniel lifts his hand.

He looks at the sleek Mercedes then back at me. The exhaust from the engine puffs into the cold morning air and hangs in front of us. I hug my backpack to my chest.

"You're sure—"

"Good luck," I say at the same time.

He narrows his eyes and studies me. I keep my smile in place.

For some reason, I didn't expect things to end so abruptly. But that's how life is sometimes, things happen or end without any notice at all.

Nathaniel holds out his hand for me to shake. "Right. Good luck, Izzy. It's been...interesting."

My chest feels all achy looking at his hand hanging there between us.

"Yup. This is it, I guess." I set down my bag and place my hand in his.

His fingers are warm and his grip is firm. Neither of us shakes. "Well, goodbye then."

I hate goodbyes.

I say with as much cheer as I can, "Let's not say bye. Let's say, 'til we meet again."

He shakes his head. "Let's just say goodbye."

"Or 'til we meet again," I add.

He keeps shaking his head no, but there's humor in his eyes.

I grin at him. "Are you sure you want to go? 'Cause it looks like you might prefer sitting on the bus next to me. I could sing one hundred bottles of beer on the wall the whole way there. Plus, I can get us vending machine coffee in the station and snacks for the ride."

He gets a mock horrified look on his face and holds up his hands in front of him like he's warding me off. "Bye, Izzy. You take care."

I nod my head quickly and try to swallow down the lump in my throat. "I will."

Then Nathaniel climbs into the car and shuts the door.

I don't wait to see if he looks at me as they drive away.

No sir.

I turn around and start walking.

I have twenty-two cents, some used paperbacks, a

notebook and two pens, a bunch of dirty clothes, and an expired bus ticket.

I don't have time to worry about Nathaniel or signs from the universe.

I need to figure out a way to get myself to Romeo.

**10**

———

My phone rings its little cricket ringtone as I walk toward the train station. I pull it out of my pack and check the display. It's my Aunt Gerry. I take a second to compose myself and then answer.

"Hi Auntie."

I smile when I hear barking in the background.

Aunt Gerry has two long-haired wiener dogs that are just about the sweetest little dogs in the world. But every time she gets on the phone they bark incessantly. It's like they don't want her paying attention to anyone but them.

"Izzy, where are you, sweetie?" she asks over the barking.

At her voice, a flood of happiness comes over me. Aunt Gerry is my dad's sister. She took over raising me when I was eleven.

"I'm in Albany. How are Oscar and Meyer?" I ask after her dogs.

"Loud," she says, then, "why in the world are you in Albany? There's nothing up there. I thought you were coming to stay for a bit."

I hum noncommittally into the phone. Aunt Gerry lives in a sweet little apartment in Queens. My childhood bedroom is still decorated with the white wicker furniture and stuffed animals she picked out for me when I first arrived. I never had the heart to change the décor because it reminded me of how much she loved me and wanted me to be happy. It's been nearly ten years since I've lived with her, but I used to come and stay weekends every now and then. Although, I haven't done that in nearly a year.

Almost like she can read my thoughts she says, "it's been a year, Izzy."

"I know."

The dogs bark a little louder and I wait until they calm down before I say, "I just need to do something first. Then I'll come."

"Do what?" Aunt Gerry doesn't like to be kept out of the loop.

I drop my backpack to the asphalt and stare at the train station. "I'm just...I'm gonna head up to Romeo."

My chest clenches as I wait to hear what Aunt Gerry has to say. Like "that's trouble Isabella" or "why can't you just let the past go" or "Izzy, why oh why do you go chasing trouble" but she doesn't.

Instead, she says, "To see David?"

My throat is tight. "Yeah."

"Well, it's about time I suppose," she says prosaically. "You can't keep running forever."

"I'm not running," I say. But my words are hollow, because what else do you call quitting your job, leaving your friends and family behind, and traveling the world?

"You should see Erma while you're there," says Aunt Gerry, which is a completely different path than I thought she'd go.

"I'm not gonna see Erma. I'm not interested."

"Because of David?"

I don't say anything. The dogs bark a bit and Aunt Gerry shushes them.

I pick up my backpack and sling it over my shoulder. Even though the sun has come up, the air is still chilly, and the brick and glass train station looks warm and inviting. I start walking across the parking lot toward the front entrance.

Then I reiterate, "I'm not interested."

Aunt Gerry sighs and I hear her moving to the kitchen and sorting through the cupboard. By the tinkling sounds, I know she's pulled down the tea kettle and a tea cup and saucer. A wave of longing rushes over me. What I'd give to sit in her tiny kitchen, at the table next to the small white stove, and have a cup of her too-hot chamomile tea.

"I worry about you, Izzy," she says in a moment of candid seriousness.

I stop at the entrance to the train station and admit with equal candor, "I worry about me too."

After that bit of honesty, there isn't much to say.

"You're out of money?" she asks.

"Yup," I admit. It took a little less than a year of unemployment to work through my savings.

"Let me send you some."

"Nah, I'll be fine. I've got some things I can sell. It just has to last a few days longer. It'll be fun."

There's a pause in the conversation. Years ago, I used my annual bonus to pay off the rest of her mortgage. I think she feels an unnecessary debt to me. But I didn't help her to get anything in return, just like she didn't expect anything in return when she took me when I was little.

"You take care of yourself. If you need anything, call. You hear?" she says, reasserting her bossy auntie persona.

"Yes, ma'am," I say.

She snorts. "See you soon."

I hang up and then sink to the asphalt.

The fall sunshine hasn't warmed the ground yet, so it's cold, even through my jeans. I lean back against the brick wall of the station and stare at the voicemail notification on my phone. My finger hovers over it and my hand shakes. There's a message on there from David.

I let out a long sigh and shove my phone into my backpack.

"Come on, Izzy," I whisper. "Chin up. You can do it. The universe sent you a sign, and Aunt Gerry called, and—"

"I leave you on your own for fifteen minutes and you end up on the ground talking to yourself."

I startle at the unexpected voice and look up. A happy, elated feeling settles over me.

He's here. He came back.

"You just couldn't keep away," I say. The cloud of worry and tension that was hanging over me disappears.

I squint up at Nathaniel. The sun is behind him and I can only make out his tall figure, broad shoulders and dark hair.

"Look at you. You're no good at goodbyes either," I say.

He isn't smiling, but when I peek at his expression I can tell he's happy to see me too.

"I thought you had your fancy schmancy ride to Romeo? Did your colleague kick you to the curb? Poor Nate." I grin at him, I'm so, so happy to see him I could hug him. I thought I could do it on my own, but it feels so much easier with him here.

"Don't call me Nate," he says, then he frowns at me.

"I missed your scowl." I hold out my hand for him to help me up. He shakes his head and then fits his hand in mine and pulls me to my feet. He keeps ahold of my hand for a second after he lifts me up, then scowls at me again and lets go.

I'm feeling much more positive about everything. "So, tell me the truth. You came back because you realized your life is empty, dull and lifeless without me." I fit my backpack over my shoulders and bounce on my toes.

"Hardly." He scoffs and pulls the cuffs of his flannel shirt over his wrists. He's still in farmer Tom's outfit. Although I'm still rocking my dirty jeans and sweater, so I guess we match.

He clears his throat and then studies me. "Just to be clear, I only came back because..."

He pauses and his eyebrows draw down. He gives me a

funny look, like he's trying to work out a puzzle but can't seem to figure it out.

"Because....?" I ask when he doesn't say anything more.

"Because...you..." He frowns. Then he says more quietly, "I didn't want you to be on your own. It didn't feel right leaving you."

That's alright because it didn't feel right him leaving. But instead of saying so, I smirk up at him.

"You like my brand of fun, don't you?"

He shakes his head. "I'm terrified of your brand of fun."

I grin at him and nudge his arm with my shoulder. He's tall. Although, I only really notice it when we're standing this close together. In fact, we're close enough that I can feel the heat coming off of him. I'm cold from sitting on the pavement, so I step a little closer to him.

"So, what're you up for? Hitchhiking? Panhandling to gather enough for bus tickets? Street performing for cash? If you can dance I can do cartwheels."

"Wait...you don't have a ticket? Or a ride?" He gives me an appalled look.

I press my lips together and look at him innocently.

"How were you going to get to Romeo?" he asks. He runs his hand through his hair in frustration. It gets a little bit messy and ruffled. It makes him look more human.

"I told you...I'd get there by hitchhiking or the bus. Do you have a preference?"

"Unbelievable." He looks around the parking lot at all the parked cars then at the doors of the train station. The ticket counter for the bus is inside.

"So...the bus?" I say brightly.

"You're lucky I came back," he says.

"Why's that?" I ask, even though I agree with him.

"Because I have enough money for tickets."

I hold back a smile. "I could've made the money. Like I said, I once sang—"

"I know. The whole of *Cats* to make enough money-"

"Including the song *Memory,* which was really hard—"

"Izzy, I don't dance and I won't hitchhike. The tickets are only eight dollars. I'll buy yours too-"

"I'm not helpless—" I say.

"And I'll get you lunch."

I stop talking, and so does he. We stare at each other. His eyes are challenging and I feel a little bit out of breath. Still, I tilt my chin up and put on a stubborn stare to match his stern, no-nonsense expression.

Finally I ask, "Did you say lunch?"

The side of his mouth almost quirks up. "I did. I bet there's food inside the station. Maybe a croissant."

Hmmm.

"You're right," I nudge his arm with my elbow, "I'm extremely lucky you came back."

He nods toward the front entrance. "Come on then. I want to get to Romeo as soon as possible. Our love lives depend on it."

Ah. Right.

I was hungry, but the thought of Romeo and love ruins my appetite.

# 11

Izzy

THE SUN IS HIGH AND SHINING BRIGHTLY ON DOWNTOWN Romeo.

I hop down from the bus onto the curb and turn back to make sure Nathaniel is climbing down after me. He's a lot more composed than I am. He thanks the driver and then steps to the pavement. The bus door swings shut and then the bus puffs away in a cloud of exhaust. Romeo is just one of many stops on its route.

I squint after it and then take in the town.

Romeo, New York, Official Town of Love.

I frown at the cute storefronts painted bright colors like lemon yellow, baby blue and strawberry red. Lining the sidewalk are pots of yellow, red and orange chrysanthemums, haybales, pumpkins and cornstalks.

There's even a scarecrow outside the old timey hardware store.

The town is adorable, and I used to love its adorableness. Heck, I was going to live here. Get married, have kids, spend my life here. I was totally won over by its small-town, friendly charm.

Today the bronze Juliet statue, the cute bakery, the flowers, the happy people waving to each other as they pass on the street, it doesn't win me over. It just hurts. Sort of like when you've been inside a dark room and then you walk outside on a clear sunny day. At noon.

It hurts your eyes so much that you have to close them.

Nathaniel turns in a slow circle and takes everything in. "I always meant to come here." He looks over at me. "Is it the same as the last time you were here?"

I shake my head. "The last time I was here I was in a church. That one." I point at a stone church with a steeple not far from downtown. "It looks the same."

He stares at me for a moment, then the confused look on his face clears. "Ah. The wedding that didn't work out."

I nod. "Something like that."

I hitch my backpack onto my shoulders.

Nathaniel looks toward the softly rounded mountain outside of town. There's a small woodland resort there. It has skiing in the winter and hiking in the summer, and of course, weddings. Lots and lots of weddings. I bet that's where Gertrude and Raphael are staying.

I can tell Nathaniel is chomping at the bit to rush up there and rescue Gertrude. I'm not sure it's going to turn out exactly like he hopes, but stranger things have happened.

"Thank you again," I say. "For the ticket. For the croissant. For...everything."

He waves his hand like it was nothing. And maybe to him it was nothing, but to me it meant more than he could ever know.

"Good luck with everything," he says.

"You too." And then on impulse I throw my arms around him. At first he's stiff, just as stiff as usual, but then slowly, he relaxes and he hugs me back. My big backpack only sort of gets in the way.

After a few seconds I pull away.

And because I really, really hate goodbyes I say, "Well, what're you waiting for? Is this the town of love or isn't it? Go on. Go get your girl."

So he does.

**12**

———————

Nathaniel

"I *am* Nathaniel Barry. I made the reservation for three nights. You can see it here on my laptop."

I try to keep my voice even and not let the frustration I'm feeling show. I'm trying to check in at the Woodlands Resort, and it's not going well.

I hold my computer screen up for the receptionist to see. She has scraped-back black hair that matches her black dress.

"I'm sorry, sir, it's resort policy. You must present ID upon check-in."

I set my computer down on the check-in desk and rub my temples. I was so relieved to find my briefcase and laptop at the train station's lost and found that I didn't even think about needing an ID for check-in. I would've asked my colleague for more than a quick loan if I'd known this was going to happen.

The receptionist's lips are pinched and her arms are folded across her chest. She's definitely not going to budge.

I wonder what Izzy would do in this situation.

I shake my head at the thought. What's wrong with me? She'd make trouble, that's what she'd do.

Or tell a story about her granny, or...I narrow my eyes. Maybe Izzy was actually onto something.

"I'm sorry about this," I begin again.

The receptionist shrugs. "It's policy. You can't stay without ID."

"Sure. On my way here I was mugged—"

"Oh. Oh no. That's awful!" Her hand flies to her chest and she gives me a more sympathetic look.

I nod and try to play up her sympathy. The only other place to stay in Romeo is a B&B and they're all booked up. I *have* to stay here. Also, this is where Gertrude is. I have a better chance of finding her if we're in the same hotel.

I hold my hands out disarmingly. "So you see, I don't have any ID to show you. But..."

She nods encouragingly.

"I do know someone that lives in town who could vouch that I am who I say I am."

The receptionist's brow wrinkles and I can tell she's chewing this over. "Well...maybe. Who do you know?"

I give a bland smile. "Miss Erma."

The change is instant. The formerly unmovable receptionist gives me a happy, toothy smile. "Oh, Miss Erma.

Well, that's a different story. Of course that would work. Miss Erma. Isn't that wonderful?"

I keep my expression flat. I almost forgot that Miss Erma has superstar level status in this town.

She was my grandma's neighbor growing up, and although my grandma died more than twenty years ago, Miss Erma still chats with my mom at least once a month. Whenever Erma comes down to New York for a Broadway show or a museum trip she swings by to see my parents. Every now and then I'm there too. She always jokingly pinches my cheek and tells me someday she'll "see" my soul mate.

I always told her I'd already found my soul mate in Gertrude.

The receptionist has her phone out. It's ringing in on a video call. After a few rings Miss Erma picks up. All we can see is her ear.

"Miss Erma, hello? It's Virginia at the Woodlands Resort."

"Virginia. Hello. Did I win a free stay? See Wanda, I told you I was going to win. I saw it in a dream."

I hold back a chuckle. Wanda is Erma's best friend. By the sound of the background noise they're at some sort of jazzercise or Zumba class.

"You can't prognosticate winnings, Erma. That's horse crap," Wanda says.

"Who says I can't learn new skills late in life?" Erma replies. She shifts the phone to her other ear. We catch a quick glimpse of a dance studio, lots of mirrors and about a dozen older women shimmying around.

"Psychic dreaming isn't a skill you can just learn," argues Wanda.

Virginia's pale face turns bright red. "No, no. Miss Erma, I'm sorry. You didn't win, Elliot Driver won. We're on video. Can you hold the phone up so we can see you?"

"Elliot Driver? I definitely didn't see that," she says. Then she mutters, "We who? Who's on video?"

She fumbles with the phone. It flips upside down for a second and then Erma's and Wanda's faces fill the screen.

"Why, Nathaniel, what are you doing in Romeo?" Erma gives me a big, grandmotherly smile.

I glance over at Virginia and quirk an eyebrow as if to say, "see, I'm Nathaniel."

"Maybe he also won the free stay from the drawing," Wanda says. "You didn't see that coming, did you?"

Erma shoos Wanda away and walks to the opposite side of the studio, away from the dancing ladies.

"Miss Erma, I just needed you to confirm that this is Nathaniel Barry," Virginia says.

Erma scoffs. "Of course he's Nathaniel Barry, who else would he be?"

"Thank you," I say warmly. Now I can check in, use the room phone to call Gertrude, find her and convince her—

"Nathaniel, I just called your mother this morning."

A twinge of guilt hits me. For the past few months Erma has asked after me. My mom said that she'd been feeling down lately. Her godson recently died and for some reason Erma claims that I remind her of him. My mom kept asking me to go and pay her a visit to cheer her up.

I never did.

"I've finally seen your soul mate."

I frown at the screen. "Excuse me?"

Virginia gasps. "That's so wonderful." She turns the full force of her enthusiasm on me. "Do you know what that means? You're going to fall in love and get married and live happily ever after!"

"I'm already in love," I tell Virginia.

"Oh." She frowns and looks back to the video call.

Erma gives me a pleased look. "She's in Romeo right now." Her brown eyes crinkle with amusement.

The back of my neck itches and I get the horrible feeling that she's about to say my soul mate is Izzy.

"She's an accountant," Erma says in the same way a magician would say "ta da!"

I let out a relieved sigh. Not Izzy. Not Izzy at all.

She's talking about Gertrude. Of course she is. I've always known that Gertrude and I are perfect together.

"That's great," I say. "I knew it. I already knew it. That's perfect. Thank you, Erma."

Virginia puts her free hand to her chest and goes, "Awwwww."

Erma's tilts her head and studies at me like a bird watching a worm. "You've seen her already?"

"Not yet." I shake my head. "But she's staying here too. I'll find her. I'll get her back."

The music in the dance studio changes to a faster, more upbeat song.

"Erma, it's your song," shouts Wanda.

Erma lifts her eyebrows and her eyes twinkle. "It looks like I'm needed."

"Bye, Miss Erma," Virginia says.

"Thank you," I say.

Erma gives me a wink. "I'm pleased about your soul mate, Nathaniel. I knew you'd like her. She's respectable, smart, demure. She fits you perfectly."

I nod, but I can't manage to say anything in response.

Before, if I lost Gertrude to Raphael I'd be broken-hearted. Now, the stakes are even higher, because if I lose Gertrude, I've lost my soul mate.

**13**

***

NATHANIEL

GERTRUDE DOESN'T ANSWER HER PHONE. SO I WASTE FIVE hours wandering the resort, the town, every romantic location I can think of trying to find her.

She's not in the rose garden, the park, the chocolate shop, the bakery or the quaint Italian restaurant. She's not at any of the activities at the resort.

I shove aside the thought that I can't find her because she's holed up in her hotel room spending hours in bed with Raphael. That's not a thought I'm going to entertain.

Especially because the rooms here are perfect honeymoon fare. The beds are huge and comfortable, with white down comforters and piles of pillows. The furniture is dark walnut and romantically ornate. The white curtains are sheer and billowy. There's a fireplace in every room and a jacuzzi tub in the bathroom. There's even a bottle of local wine and a box of chocolates on the desk as a welcome gift. It's like the room was designed to inspire meals in bed, romantic toasts, and long bouts of love-making that alternate between the bed and the jacuzzi.

I scowl at the lobby chandelier, it's made of hundreds of heart crystals that send little prism rainbows dancing in front of me. Somehow, the Woodlands Resort managed to combine the love and romanticism of Romeo with enthusiasm for the outdoors. Wood paneling, hiking and ski décor blend perfectly with sheer white fabrics, flower bouquets and crystal hearts.

There's a tight panicky feeling in my chest. Gertrude and I were together for three years. We had plans. We had a past and a future. No, we have. We have a future.

It's closing in on Friday night. She said she was getting married on Sunday. I can't let that happen. If she marries Raphael, not only will I lose my soul mate, so will she. Erma may have doubters about the accuracy of her predictions, but I'm not one of them.

There's a couple kissing on a beige damask couch near the lobby fireplace. The woman has auburn hair just the color of Gertrude's. The man she's with looks Greek or maybe Italian. He could be a Raphael. I stalk over.

"Excuse me..."

They look up. Curious but not guilty. Because it's not Gertrude.

"Sorry. I thought you were someone else."

I decide to head back to my room. I'll try her cell again from the room phone.

As I head toward the elevators I hear a loud, hoarse laugh. I stop walking. I hear the laugh again. It's Gertrude. I'd recognize her laugh anywhere. She always told me it embarrassed her because it sounds like a mix between a hyena and a donkey. It never bothered me, but because it embarrassed her so much she barely laughed out loud.

There it is again.

I hurry toward the sound. She must be dining in the café off the lobby. It's a little restaurant with soups, salads, sandwiches, and lots of desserts. When I first saw it I stopped for a moment because the dessert display case had chocolate croissants and I wondered for a second if Izzy liked chocolate croissants. Then I wondered why I was still thinking about Izzy.

The dessert case is also full of towering cakes, pies, puddings, crème puffs, profiteroles, and chocolate mousse.

I can only imagine that Raphael is plying Gertrude with dessert after dessert to sweeten her up. I scowl at the thought. No more.

This is it. As soon as Gertrude sees me, the weird Raphael spell will be broken and she'll come back to New York.

I storm into the café, past the surprised hostess. There are two dozen round tables with long white tablecloths. Nearly all the tables are full. I sweep my gaze over the room. Where is she? I don't see her. I don't—

I see her.

And I stop, like a deer caught in the headlights. Because that's not Gertrude. I mean, it is. But it isn't. She's in a tight red dress with a low neckline. Her auburn hair is piled high in a sexy style. Her head is thrown back and she's laughing.

That's not all.

The man with her. Raphael. He's... Izzy was right.

He has shoulder-length blond hair tied back from his face and the square leonine features of a Nordic Olympian. The guy's dripping testosterone. He looks like he just skied down the Alps, rescued a village of virgins, and then built a stone castle with his bare hands. He's watching Gertrude with a smug, propriety expression. One hand is on her thigh and his other hand is resting over hers on the table. Then I see the ring. A big, fat, flashy diamond engagement ring.

I can't move. I can't think. They're all cozied up. Raphael leans toward Gertrude and whispers something in her ear. Then he runs his hand down her throat.

My mouth goes dry and my heart sounds loud in my ears.

The conversations of the diners, the clinking noise of a waiter carrying a large silver dessert tray loaded with mousse and crème puffs, all of that fades. Raphael picks up Gertrude's hand and kisses her fingers one by one until he comes to the engagement ring, then he kisses that too.

My body goes cold. I can't look away. I can't even move. Then, Gertrude finally looks toward where I'm standing.

I don't think, I panic. She can't see me. Not here, not like this, not with Raphael the love-machine in his element and me dressed in farmer Tom's cast-offs.

I take a quick step back. But I forgot about the waiter and his dessert tray. He's behind me. I hit him hard. He lets out a sharp oomph. The dishes rattle. The tray wobbles. The waiter's expression goes from calm to panic as I pinwheel backward, hit the tray with my arms, and flip it over.

The chocolate mousse, the tiny finger cakes, the pile of profiteroles catapult into the air and then rain down on me like mini dessert grenades. I slam into the floor, the silver tray smacks me, and pastries and mousse splatter over me.

"No! The crème puffs!" the waiter yells. "You ruined the crème puffs!"

I swipe the pastries off my face and scramble out from beneath the tray. "Sorry," I say. "Sorry."

Then I frantically glance around the tables. Gertrude's standing now, peering over the diners. I can hear her. She gestures toward the furious waiter.

"I think I saw Nathaniel," she says shrilly.

Oh no.

Raphael tugs at her hand. "Sit down, my treasure. It's not him."

"No. I think I saw him."

I don't wait to hear more. I army crawl across the floor, staying low and moving fast. My face is covered in chocolate mousse and my hair is full of crème puffs. This is not the moment I need Gertrude to see me. Cake-covered Nathaniel versus romance Raphael isn't a contest.

I crawl under a table with two older ladies in fur coats. They squeal and kick at me with their sharp high heels until I flee out the other side.

"It was him, I swear," Gertrude says.

"You said Nathaniel is urbane. That man was an uncouth farmer." Raphael again.

The waiter with the dessert tray is still fuming, and

Gertrude is still peering around the room, convinced she saw me. There's another table in the corner with only one person sitting at it. I dive for the tablecloth and crawl under.

I take a second to slow my breathing and wait for something to go terribly wrong. Either the woman at the table above me will start kicking me and screaming about perverts, or Gertrude will pull up the tablecloth and say "it is you" and Raphael will smugly win her for good. Or...

"Excuse me, I think my boyfriend is under your table."

I hold extremely still and crouch in a little ball under the round wooden table. The white tablecloth nearly touches the floor, but I can see the tip of Gertrude's high heels and Raphael's brown wingtips behind her.

"If you don't mind, I'm just going to look."

I close my eyes. How did my life come to this? How did I go from an incredibly successful, well-respected businessman to a disaster covered in cake crouched under a table? It's embarrassing.

I wait for the tablecloth to lift up, but it doesn't.

I move back but the woman at the table kicks me. I grunt and then hold still.

*Wait a minute.*

I recognize those shoes.

"Don't you dare," a woman with a southern drawl a mile wide says. "My husband is under this table giving me the French tickle, it's our honeymoon, and I always wanted a little tongue bath in public. Ah ah. Back away from the tablecloth, missy."

A grin spreads across my face. She's absurd, she's obscene, she's the best.

I could kiss her.

"If you lift this tablecloth this whole restaurant and all them old ladies will see my hoo-ha. That'll ruin their appetites. Or it'll make 'em jealous. Either way."

"Uh...uh...what?"

"My treasure," Raphael says, "the lady says the man you saw is her husband."

"But...but I swear I saw Nathaniel. I don't know why he's here. I told him not to come," Gertrude says.

"Well, that settles it. You couldn't have seen a Nathaniel. My husband's name is Devon."

I stifle a surprised laugh and Izzy kicks at me again.

"Now, if you'll please excuse us, I'd like to get back to it. We only live once, ya know."

Wow.

She's crazy.

She's perfect.

She rescued me.

I let out a long sigh of relief as Gertrude and Raphael's shoes disappear from my line of sight.

I sit quietly and ponder the absurdity of life while I wait for Izzy to give me the all clear. Finally, she sticks her head under the table. The tablecloth falls around her shoulders and she gives me a big grin.

"You're outta your league. Did you see that Raphael? Hubba hubba."

I give her a stern frown. "Where's David?"

She wrinkles her nose. "I already saw him. I'm more concerned about you."

I'm pretty concerned about me too.

"Miss?" It's the waiter. Izzy's eyes widen.

"Just a sec," she whispers to me.

She yanks her head back up and lowers the tablecloth.

"Mhhm. Mhhm. Right. Do you have chocolate croissants? Oh good. I'll take two. Make that four. No, five. Mhmm. You can send them up to my room with the bill...my room number? Hang on."

Izzy ducks her head back under the table. "What's our room number?"

I cough in surprise and then say, "Excuse me?"

She smiles in delight. "Face it, Nate. You need me. Where are we staying?"

I stare into her bright blue eyes and she stares right back. There's a mischievous glint in her expression.

"Two days with me and Gertrude will be back in your arms. Trust me."

"Two days? She's getting married Sunday," I say with a scowl.

"To *you*," Izzy says. "Stick with me, kid, I'll steer you right."

The funny thing is, I believe her. I underestimated Raphael, the entire situation. I need an expert.

Apparently, Izzy is an expert.

I narrow my eyes. "What do you get out of this?"

She gives me a cheeky grin. "The joy of helping a fellow human being in need? I figure fate got us together for a reason. How's that?"

Right. Whatever.

The truth is, I don't have much choice here. Desperate times call for...Izzy apparently.

"Alright, deal. You've got two days."

A wide grin spreads over Izzy's face. "Easy peasy." Then she adds, "What's your room number? I really want those croissants."

I give her a hard stare, then I say, "315. Order a bottle of wine too. And soup and sandwiches." I lick my face. "And the chocolate mousse, it's really good."

She laughs and then pops back up to get our dinner.

**14**

———

Izzy

"Is this the honeymoon suite?" I ask, turning in a slow circle.

Nathaniel's room is gorgeous. It's all white and fluffy and romantic. It's like I just stepped into a cloud. The bed is massive and has about twenty pillows piled high against the headboard.

"No," says Nathaniel. He closes the door and walks in behind me. "It's just a regular room."

"Riiight." I look at the bed. "At least there's enough pillows for you to build your wall."

Nathaniel makes a noise, sort of half choke, half pained groan. "Don't you have someplace else to spend the nights?"

I frown and look away from him. No, I don't. Not really.

Not that he needs to know that. So I smile at him and say, "'Course I do. That's not the point."

I sit back on the bed and bounce a bit. It's fluffy, and soft, and doesn't creak like the farmhouse bed.

Nathaniel scowls. It looks funny, because he's still slathered in frosting and cake crumbs and there's mousse on his face and streaked through his hair. It's real hard to look disapproving when you're covered in dessert.

"What is the point then?" He crosses his arms over his chest and gives me a stern look.

Hmm.

"The point is, I have less than forty-eight hours to make you into a swoon-worthy, panty-melting, heartthrob and I'm going to need every single second I can get. 'Cause—"

I wave my hands at him.

For a second I think he's going to argue, but then he looks down at himself and nods. "That's fair."

I cross my legs and smile at him. "You thought it was going to be easy, didn't you?"

I drop my smile when Nathaniel turns his back and pulls off his cake-covered flannel shirt.

My mouth goes dry.

Holy...

"What're you doing?" I'm embarrassed that my voice comes out all high-pitched and breathy.

He looks back at me over his shoulder. His square, firm jaw seems softer when it's plastered in buttercream frosting.

"Getting cleaned up. We're starting tonight, right?"

Oh. Ohhh.

"Mhmm. After we have dinner."

His shoulders are broader than I imagined. He rolls them and the muscles on his back ripple. Seeing his bare skin is making me itchy and uncomfortable. I squirm a bit on the bed.

There's a tattoo of a dragon on his right shoulder. Who would've ever guessed? Stern, serious Nathaniel with a tattoo.

I follow the muscles of his back down to the edge of his jeans.

I lick my lips and try to get moisture back into my mouth.

Nathaniel drops his shirt to the floor. It makes a soft rustling sound. This is too intimate, too...much. My skin's all hot and itchy and I don't want it to be.

"What's the dragon tattoo about?" I ask in a blatant attempt to distract myself.

He turns around and I try really, really hard not to look at his bare chest. I keep my eyes on the glob of chocolate mousse on his right cheek.

"I'm in finance," he says, like this should be all the explanation I need.

"Okay?"

"Dragons like gold," he says slowly.

I snort. "Was that a joke? Do you have a joke tattooed on your back?"

He lifts an eyebrow at me and I grin. "I've never seen you laugh. You can barely manage a half-smile yet you have a joke tattooed on your back? That's priceless."

I think he's suppressing a smile, so I grin big enough for the both of us. I look into his eyes and he holds my gaze, at first we're just enjoying the moment, but then something shifts and I become acutely aware that I'm sitting on a big bed and Nathaniel is half undressed and...

He breaks eye contact and looks away. "Gertrude is my soul mate."

I shake my head at the abrupt change of topic. "What?"

"Gertrude. She's my soul mate. The woman I'm supposed to end up with."

"What?" Is he warning me off?

"This town, it has a sort of soul mate psychic—"

I frown at him. "Yeah. Miss Erma. I know."

He looks at me in surprise. I shrug. "I met her once." It wasn't a happy occasion. Which is one of the reasons I'm not keen to see her again.

He nods, accepting that I'm on board the soul mate train. "Well, Gertrude is my soul mate. I thought you should know."

My chest pinches and I resist the urge to scowl. "Why would that matter to me? It's not like I'm going to fall in love with you."

Nathaniel gives me a searching look, like he knows about the itch I was feeling. I keep my face expressionless.

"I'm not interested in you that way," I reiterate.

"Because you love David?"

"Exactly." I stand up and walk to the window. The room is too small. "Don't worry about me. I'm not in danger of falling for you. If anyone should worry, it's you."

"Really?"

I turn and hold open my arms jokingly. "Two more days of this? How will you resist?"

He scoffs and looks away. "I'm going to shower off." He heads toward the bathroom.

"Good idea," I call after him. I plop back down on the cushy bed. "What are you doing?" I whisper to myself.

He leaves the bathroom door open a crack. I can see the edge of his back in the mirror. I tell myself not to look, but then he unbuttons his pants and steps out of them.

My eyes widen.

Nathaniel doesn't wear underwear. I can see the muscles of his back, his long, lean legs. There are two dimples on his sacrum and his legs are dusted with dark hair. He's gorgeous. He's...wow. I grasp the duvet in my hands. There's a line of chocolate mousse down the back of his neck. I have the sudden urge to lick it.

Gah.

I drop my eyes to the carpet and sharply exhale.

What am I doing? What am I doing? What am I doing?

I went to see David. It was hard. More than hard.

When I asked the universe for help, Nathaniel showed up. When I was feeling rock bottom today after seeing David, Nathaniel showed up again. I don't believe in coincidences.

I think I'm here to help Nathaniel get Gertrude back and he's here to help me get over David. There's no other way to look at it.

The sound of the shower is soothing, like a soft rainstorm, and the pillows smell like lavender. I lean back on the bed and close my eyes.

"So, what's your plan?"

I jerk upright in bed and let out an unladylike cussword. "You scared me."

I glare at Nathaniel. His chest is still bare, but his bottom half is wrapped in a white towel. He took the time to shave with the hotel razor, and his hair is wet and glistening. He looks good in a towel. Really, really good.

Okay, it's time to admit it. I'm physically attracted to Nathaniel. Very physically attracted. Which is a good thing. I've not felt a single spark for any man since David. This is progress. And it's completely, one hundred percent safe to feel this way because Nathaniel only wants Gertrude. This is good.

"Put some clothes on," I say.

He holds out his hands. "They're dirty."

Oh.

There's a knock at the door. I push Nathaniel into the bathroom. "You stay there."

I open the door to room service. The server has a tray piled high with soup, sandwiches, croissants, a bottle of wine and chocolate mousse. The tray smells like leeks and potatoes and melted cheese and chocolate. This is going to be good.

"Will that be all?"

My eyes go wide at the feast. "You bet. Thank you."

After he's gone I yank open the bathroom door. "Get out here. We can strategize while we eat."

**15**

———————

"So what's the plan?" Nathaniel asks.

He's dressed again in his dirty clothes. I tried to wipe off the majority of the cake and frosting, but there are still noticeable splotches on his shirt and pants.

We're strategically stationed, aka hiding, behind an autumn display of cornstalks, a scarecrow, haybales and gourds on the far side of the lobby.

Raphael and Gertrude are snuggling on a couch in front of the fireplace. They have a bottle of wine and a plate of chocolates. I narrow my eyes, Raphael has skills, no doubt about it.

"Here's the deal," I say in a quiet voice.

Even though Gertrude and Raphael are nearly a hundred feet away and separated from us by the check-in desk, the elevator bank and plenty of couples and families walking through, I don't want them to hear or catch sight of us. Not yet at least.

"You're going up against a master." I point at Raphael. He's twirling a strand of Gertrude's hair and looking at her hungrily. "Think of him as the Einstein of seduction."

"Ridiculous," Nathaniel says.

But then he narrows his eyes and pushes a cornstalk to the side as Raphael rubs his finger over Gertrude's lips, captures a drop of wine and sticks his finger in his mouth.

"That's it, I'm going out there," he says angrily. He stalks around the haybales. I grab his shirt and tug.

"No you don't," I say.

"This is ridiculous. He's going to take his hands off my girlfriend—"

He walks forward and I hang onto the back of his shirt with two hands. I slide across the floor, my shoes squeaking. "Stop right there."

"Izzy, let go."

"No, you're not ready."

He pulls forward again. I don't let go of his shirt.

He tugs.

I pull.

He tugs again.

Then, his shirt tears straight up the back. It rips right in two. I can see the skin of his back and even the dragon tattoo on his shoulder.

Nathaniel stops walking. He turns around, a shocked look on his face. "Are you kidding?"

I hold up my hands, "Sorry?" Sorry isn't cutting it. "I can sew it for you, I'm really good with a needle."

"No."

Ummm. I point back at the haybales. "Oh look, there's a scarecrow, you could trade shirts."

He glances at the scarecrow's flannel shirt, uncannily similar to the one from farmer Tom, only uglier. "Izzy. No."

I flatten my mouth to restrain a smile. "It looks like it'd fit."

He grabs my arms and pulls me back behind the haybales. "Izzy, forget it. I can't keep hiding and skulking. I need to go over there and—"

I start unbuttoning the scarecrow's shirt.

"What are you doing?"

I wink at him. "You needed a clean shirt anyway. Take yours off."

"Izzy, anyone could look over here. Gertrude could look over here."

I shake my head. "We're behind a stack of haybales. No one can see. Stop being a grandma."

I toss the shirt at him. He catches it and shakes his head at me. But instead of arguing more he strips out of his torn shirt and puts the scarecrow's shirt on. He hands back his old shirt and I work on redressing the scarecrow.

"I'm going over there," he says as he finishes buttoning the flannel.

Surprisingly, it fits pretty well and doesn't look half bad. Except for the straw poking out of the sleeves and neck, that looks a little weird, but hey, at least it's not ripped and stained.

He turns to leave. I reach for him.

"Stop. It won't work. Look at them." I point across the lobby. "That, right there. Look at them."

Nathaniel looks. His eyes darken and he clenches his jaw. Probably because Raphael is feeding Gertrude grapes like he's her love slave. I continue, "While you were skulking under my table in the café—"

Nathaniel folds his arms across his chest. "Ahem."

I try again. "While you were strategically stationed under my table in the café-"

He nods. "Better."

"I did a bit of reconnaissance, aka eavesdropping." I smile at him like "mmhmm, check my skills out." Clearly, he's not impressed. Oh well, can't win 'em all.

"Okay, here's the deal. Raphael is Italian. That means he was bottle-fed romance."

Nathaniel looks skeptical, so I continue. "When he was in diapers he was learning the skills of flirtation. At school he was fed the music and literature of love. While you were memorizing the multiplication tables, like three times three is nine, he was memorizing the three hundred and nine different ways to kiss."

"Three hundred and nine?" Nathaniel scoffs.

I nod and go on. "His language, Italian, is a *romance* language. He eats, breathes and sleeps romance. You can't go head to head with this guy, because if you try, you'll lose." I grasp for a metaphor, "it's like...you're the principal's office to his Venice."

Nathaniel gives me an affronted look. "Are you kidding? Why am I the principal's office?"

Okay, yeah, that was a terrible metaphor. "I don't know, it just popped into my head. Like, the principal never smiles, and nobody wants to go there because he spanks you."

"What?!"

I flush. That came out wrong. "I mean, he doesn't actually spank you...gah, never mind."

I turn aside and try to wipe all thoughts that involve Nathaniel, desks and spanking from my mind.

"Fine," Nathaniel says tightly. "He's some Italian Casanova. It doesn't matter, because I'm Gertrude's soul mate. That endures past seduction and romance."

I agree. I turn back to him. "Exactly. That's why my plan is going to work."

"And your plan is?"

Gertrude and Raphael are kissing now. It's that slow, leisurely, lead-up-to-wild-sex kind of kiss. Nathaniel looks a little sick to his stomach. It's definitely not the chocolate mousse we had for dessert that's making him feel ill. Poor guy.

"It's true that Raphael has seduction and charm, but you, Nathaniel...you have mystery."

He doesn't seem convinced. "I do?"

"Mhm." I put my hand on his arm. When he looks down at it, I flush, but I leave it there. He needs a little bolstering.

"You're going to drive Gertrude mad. First, you'll tease her. She'll think she hears you, but where? She can't find you. She'll think she sees you. But no, you're not there. She'll think she smells you, that woodsy cologne you wear, but you're nowhere to be found."

"I'm a mystery," he says in a flat, unimpressed voice.

"That's right. It'll drive her mad. She'll begin to question herself. If she's so happy with Raphael, then why is she hearing you, seeing flashes of you, smelling you? It must be because she still loves you. Wants you. Do you see what I mean?"

"No," he says.

I smile and pluck out some of the straw from his shirt sleeves. "Think of it this way, when you're in love, you think of your lover all the time. Even when they aren't there. Right?"

He shrugs. "Sure. I suppose."

I can't believe this. "You suppose? Weren't you ever deeply, madly, crazily in love with Gertrude? Didn't you ever feel that all-consuming tidal wave of romance?"

He frowns at me, "Izzy. Do you know what comes *after* romance?"

I sure do. "Adult diapers."

His mouth drops open in shock.

Errr. "Dementia?"

He scowls at me, apparently that wasn't it either.

"No. Respect, Izzy. Respect comes after romance."

I shake my head. "Not love?"

"Love is just another word for respect."

I try to respond to that, but honestly, words are beyond me. "That's your problem, right there. Which leads to the second part of my plan. Teaching you about romance."

Nathaniel shakes his head. "I don't need romance lessons."

I point across the lobby at Gertrude. She and Raphael

are clinking their wine glasses together. "Do you want to win Gertrude back?"

Nathaniel doesn't look at Gertrude, he just stares at me. Finally, he says, "yes."

"Then you need romance lessons. Follow my lead and in two days' time Raphael will be a distant, albeit bad memory."

Nathaniel peers around the hay bale. It isn't a pretty scene. Raphael sure does work fast.

"Fine," Nathaniel says tightly.

Good. "We start now."

**16**

———

I look at Nathaniel and think through the options. Finally I decide on one. "I'm gonna need you to laugh."

"Excuse me?"

I grin. "I know. It's probably been years. Has Gertrude ever heard you laugh?"

His eyes go distant like he's working through the years trying to locate a time when he and Gertrude laughed together. "Sure," he finally says.

"In bed?" I ask, because that would work the best.

"No."

Ugh. "Oh well. So, what you need to do is laugh *as if* you're in bed together."

"Gertrude doesn't laugh in bed. I don't laugh in bed. Why

would anyone laugh in bed?" He looks at me censoriously. Sort of like a principal might. I try not to smile.

"Okay. Well, I'll help you out. I'll give you an example. Picture this."

I lean against the hay bale. Nathaniel stands stiffly a few feet away. That's not going work. I stand up and tug on his arm, pulling him to lean beside me.

"Relax," I say.

After a second he becomes less stiff. I lean into him. The smell of hay surrounds us.

"Picture a field. It's early fall, the air is cool, but it's midday so the sun has warmed the grass enough for you to lie down. There are apple trees nearby, the apples are ripe and some of them have fallen, so the air smells crisp and sweet. There are a few farmhouses nearby, but not close enough for anyone to see you."

"What does this have to do with laughing?"

"Shhh." I shush him. "There are some bees droning overhead and a few birds hopping between the apple trees. It's the weekend. You have nowhere to go and nothing to do. Except make love. That's the only thing on your mind. Because your girl is on the soft warm grass beneath you, and her lips taste like Honeycrisp apples and she's looking at you like she wants to taste you too."

I lean closer to Nathaniel, caught up in the smell of the hay and the memory of a crisp apple. "So you slowly lift up her skirt, play your fingers over her skin, taste the apple on her mouth. And then, she lifts her half-eaten apple up to you, like Eve in the Garden. You look at the apple and then you look at her, there's a glint in her eye. You lick the apple and then you push inside her, and it feels so good, you feel so happy, that you laugh. You laugh from the joy of it… you…you…"

My throat feels tight and painful. I look down and see that my fists are clenched. I slowly, carefully release them.

"I?" Nathaniel says.

I clear my throat and try to push aside the burning, scratchiness that has lodged there.

"You laugh. That's how you laugh." Then more angrily, because he still looks like he doesn't understand, I say, "Just do it."

He shakes his head at me then stands up straight. I push away from the hay bale too and look around it at Gertrude. "Go ahead."

Nathaniel takes a deep breath and then laughs.

Gertrude didn't hear. Thank goodness. I look back at him. "That was *terrible*. You sounded like an anemic donkey."

He holds up his hands, "I can't laugh on demand."

I purse my lips. "Try again. This time do it loud enough for her to hear. But picture apples and sex and pleasure."

He rolls his shoulders, shakes out his arms, and looks, for all intents and purposes, like he's warming up for a big game. My irritation thaws. Cute. He takes a big breath, then he looks at me. Wow. I take a step back. His eyes are all dark and dripping dream boaty-ness.

"Ready," he says.

"Oookay."

He closes his eyes, lifts his head and laughs. It echoes through the lobby. Little electric tingles rush across my arms and chest. It feels like his laugh is petting me. Goodness.

I stare at him in shock.

Now that's a sexy laugh.

He stops, but I can still feel him on me, little vibrations ripple over my skin.

"How was that?"

I shake my head and try to come out of my stupor.

"Did she hear?" he asks.

Oh. Ohhh. Gertrude. I quickly peek around the hay bale. Gertrude is standing, looking around the lobby, her forehead is wrinkled and she looks confused. I smile.

Raphael grabs her hand and tries to pull her back down to the couch. She shakes her head vehemently and says something. He tries to placate her. But no, Gertrude isn't having it. She points in our direction.

Oops.

"Time to go," I say.

"But did it work?" Nathaniel asks.

"Like a charm." Then I grab his hand and rush to the side exit.

We hurry into the darkness of the resort lawn. The cool night air hits my face and helps banish the warm tinglies I was feeling.

"What happened?" asks Nathaniel as I keep pulling him down the grassy slope toward the lake.

"It worked."

"But that's good, right? Why are we running?"

"Because she's trying to find you."

He starts to slow, like he thinks it's a good idea for her to find him.

"She can't see you. Not yet. Remember? You're a mystery."

Just in case that didn't do it, I remind him, "And you look like a scarecrow."

That does it. We hurry down the slope. There's a group of rowboats by the lake. We make them just as Gertrude and Raphael open the door.

"Duck," I shove Nathaniel down and drop to the ground.

I hear Gertrude and Raphael but I can't make out their words.

"Come on, crawl under here," I say. I shimmy under the rowboat.

Thankfully, Nathaniel doesn't argue.

The space is tight, there's only about two feet of head room. The boat is about ten feet long and four feet wide. I curl up on the ground and Nathaniel crawls in next to me. We face each other, and our noses nearly touch. His breath tickles my lips. I wrap my hands around my knees and try to keep still. He lifts an eyebrow and I wink at him. There's just enough light to see each other.

After about thirty seconds, I hear Gertrude.

"I saw someone come down here."

"My treasure, it was nothing. You feel guilty, yes? But you shouldn't. This is love. You are imagining Nathaniel. You do not want him. It is guilt playing with you. Come inside. There is no one here. Even if there were, he is not worthy of you."

Nathaniel makes an angry noise, so I put my fingers to his lips. They're surprisingly soft and warm. He looks at me in surprise. I pull my fingers away like they've been burned.

"I didn't imagine it though," Gertrude says.

Her voice fades, presumably because they're walking back up to the building.

Nathaniel sighs and closes his eyes. He looks completely, utterly deflated. Probably, because he's in a scarecrow's shirt, hiding under a rowboat, and he's now covered in, I feel the ground, yup, that's mud. Oh, and his girlfriend wants to marry another man.

After a moment, the only sound is our breathing and the crickets starting their night song.

"What now?" he finally asks.

"That was good," I say. It really was. "Gertrude's starting to wonder. To question her decision."

"And?"

And I know exactly what needs to come next.

"Now it's time for a bit of romance."

**17**

———

Izzy

The rowboat oars make a sweet splashing sound as Nathaniel rows us to the middle of the little lake.

It'll only take a minute to get there. This is one of the many spring-fed mountain lakes in Upstate New York.

The literature at the resort says it's called Sunrise Lake because of how the water reflects gold and pink and orange when the sun peeks over the mountain every morning. I wouldn't know about sunrise, but right now, the full moon casts a bright, silvery reflection over the dark indigo water.

I lean to the side and peer over the boat's edge. A current flows around the boat from Nathaniel's rowing, but otherwise there aren't any waves.

The surface is opaque and placid. I shiver. There's something disconcerting about not being able to see beneath the surface. I can only see the moon and my own distorted reflection. There's no way to know what lies beneath unless you dive in. I shiver again. It's easier to stay on the surface.

I sit on a wooden plank facing Nathaniel. Our knees almost touch. He's looking out over the water, a pensive expression on his face.

The forest on the far side of the lake is dark except for the moon glistening off the peeling bark of a few silver birch trees. The night is so quiet it feels like I can hear the stars winking. Except, there's the tinkling of the waterdrops from the oars and the gentle thudding of the oars against the boat.

Nathaniel pulls the oars up and rolls his shoulders. "Well, now what?"

He leans toward me and our knees brush together. It's gentle, like when you feel the air kiss your face as a butterfly flies past. The fabric of my jeans scrapes against my skin and little goosebumps form.

I lean away from him, pull my legs back and tuck them under the hard wooden seat. Nathaniel doesn't notice.

He just asks, "Well? I rowed us to the middle of the pond. Now what?"

I guess during his pensive, thinking time, he decided that he was impatient.

"Now we do romance," I say.

He scratches his chin and looks around. Our little rowboat rocks gently when he shifts on his seat. After he's taken in the moonlight, the twinkling stars, and the dark water he turns back to me. "Alright. Train me, sensei."

I stifle a laugh. What a smart aleck. I gesture to our

surroundings. "This is Romance 101. Every man has tools that he can use to help him woo a woman. The first tool is environment."

Nathaniel nods in understanding. "Romantic, secluded lake on a moonlit night. Got it."

"Exactly. The environment does most of the work for you." To make sure he's getting my point I quiz him. "Name a few more environments that would work for this purpose."

He runs his hand through his hair and narrows his eyes in thought.

"You haven't done this before, have you?" I shake my head at him.

He shrugs. "Gertrude likes routine. We see each other twice a week. On Saturdays, we go to the same Thai place. On Wednesdays we go to the same coffee shop, she gets a latte and I get..."

He trails off, probably at the disbelieving expression on my face. "I'm sorry. Are you saying that you only see each other two nights a week? And every week you do the same thing?"

He pulls at his collar and shifts on his seat. "Yes?"

"Do you also pencil in sex?"

He tugs out a bit of straw that's still stuck in his collar. "Sure. That's on Saturdays from 6:30 to 6:45, right before dinner."

Holy unbelievable. I try to say something but nothing comes out. This is incredible. I don't know if I can fix this. He's too far gone.

Then I see the slight upturn of Nathaniel's lips and the humor in his expression.

"Ohhh. Har har," I say. "You got me."

Then, for the first time that I've ever seen, Nathaniel smiles.

Holy wow.

If smiles had the power to knock you over, then I'd be lying at the bottom of the boat. I put my hand to my chest. I can't seem to catch my breath. His eyes crinkle and dance with humor. His whole demeanor changes from serious into something playful and enticing, and I feel as if I'm caught up and being pulled toward him. I can't look away.

Thank goodness he doesn't smile more often. I wouldn't be able to survive it.

I pull in a shaky breath.

"So..." I clear my throat. "You were saying...romantic environments?"

He reels his smile back in, and once more his face is stoic and serious. I feel like I can breathe again, but weirdly, it's not the same, because now I know what he looks like when he smiles. Not like he's insanely handsome, or beautiful, or anything like that, no, it's more like a magnet that pulls me toward him and I'm powerless to resist. I don't like it. It feels like that noonday sun, uncomfortably bright sensation I felt before. I want to close my eyes against it.

He studies me for a second and then says, "Well, if I were looking for an environment to 'romance'"—he does air quotes with his fingers—"a woman, then I'd take her to...the principal's office?"

I snort and he winks at me. "Kidding. I'd take her on a picnic in the park. There are these huge flat boulders in

Central Park that you can climb on. I'd pack a picnic on a sunny day and take her there."

My chest feels sore. "Did you ever do that?" I ask wistfully.

"No. Gertrude doesn't like sitting on the ground, we never went to the park," he shrugs and the image of his picnic disappears.

I frown. "What else then. What would she like? You have to please the woman you're with. Think romantic, secluded, and intimate."

He nods and I can tell he's thinking it over. "I'd take her to the Guggenheim, right before they close. To the very top of the spiral walkway. We'd look down over the edge, it curves like the frosting on a wedding cake, and when she was dizzy from the height I would tilt her face to me and kiss her."

I sit quietly and watch as Nathaniel pictures this moment. A lone duck flies overhead, calling out in the moonlight.

"How's that?" he finally asks.

"Good," I say tersely. "Good. You can try that when you and Gertrude are back in New York. I'm sure she'll love it."

He considers this. I'm not too sure that he agrees. Maybe Gertrude won't love it. Maybe she really does like extreme routine. Except, if she does, then why is she in Romeo with Raphael?

"But first, you're in a rowboat, in the middle of a lake. So."

"Alright," Nathaniel says. "Gertrude and I are in the

romantic environment, a rowboat in the middle of the lake, now what?"

The boat rocks a bit. The stars are out in full force now and I can hear the soft lapping of the water against the rocks on the far side of the lake. I can smell the cold water and the loamy forest. Everything is exactly right.

"Kissing," I say. "Everyone should kiss in the moonlight at least once in their life."

He lifts an eyebrow.

"But first, you have to woo her with poetry. Poetry is the prelude to sex."

Nathaniel shakes his head. "Are you kidding?"

I put on my stern teacher face. "Do I look like I'm kidding?"

He considers my expression. "No," he decides. "You don't. But consider this, I'm in finance. I'm not the poetic type. Some men can write poetry, others can read balance sheets. I'm the balance sheet type."

Hah.

"I disagree. Love makes poets of us all."

I stay quiet while he considers this.

"Alright," he finally concedes.

I smile. "Okay. Stand up. Pretend you're Romeo and I'm your Juliet. Or...you know...you're you and I'm Gertrude."

I make the motion for Nathaniel to stand.

After a moment he braces himself against his seat and then rises. The boat sways in the water. He spreads his feet wide so that he doesn't capsize us or fall out of the boat. When the rocking slows he asks, "Now what?"

"Now recite me a love poem." I fold my hands in my lap

and look up at him adoringly. I even bat my eyelashes prettily for effect.

He clears his throat.

"What?" I ask.

He looks embarrassed. "I don't know any love poems."

My adoring expression falters. "Shall I compare thee to a summer's day?" I ask.

He shakes his head. "Nope."

I frown at him. "She walks in beauty like the night?"

"No."

My frown deepens to a scowl. "Oh my love is like a red, red rose, that's newly sprung in June?"

"Not ringing a bell."

Unbelievable. I narrow my eyes. "Totally not okay. We have moonlight. A rowboat and a romantic setting. Now we need poetry. Improvise." I wave my hand and reapply my adoring expression.

"Improvise?"

I nod and beam at him. "Improvise a love poem, my dear, dear Romeo."

He sighs and looks up at the moon, probably for inspiration. Then I think he's found some, because he looks back at me with a determined glint in his eye.

"Negative balance sheets are red, and positive earnings are black. You are lovely beyond compare and I really want you back."

He looks at me with a proud expression.

I hold back a horrified laugh. "What was that?"

"A poem. For an accountant."

Okay, there's no holding it in, my horrified laugh escapes. "No accountant would like that poem."

"How do you know? Are you an accountant?" he counters.

"Do I look like an accountant?" No way, no how.

His look seems to say, "not at all."

"So what do you do, exactly?" he asks.

I think about this, then say, "I travel. I experience the richness of life. I...we're not talking about me. We're talking about you and your lack of poetic finesse. You'll just have to trust me that an accountant wouldn't be impressed with your poem."

The corner of Nathaniel's lip twitches. He's holding back a smile. I know he realizes it was awful.

"Try again. One more time."

I plaster on another lovesick expression on my face. Fifteen seconds of silence pass. "Well come on. Lay it on me."

"I can't with that look on your face," he says.

"What look?"

"It's sort of a cross between a constipated chihuahua and a goldfish begging for breakfast."

I laugh. "What?"

He tries to show me what I look like. He bunches up his face and purses his lips, then blinks his eyes at me superfast. It looks ridiculous.

I snort. "I do not."

He nods. "You do."

I stick my tongue out and cross my eyes. "Better?"

"Much."

"Good. Try again."

He holds out his hands, like an actor on stage and gestures magnificently. The boat sways. "There once was a girl from...where are you from?"

I grin up at him. This is better than poetry. "Atlanta."

"There once was a girl from Atlanta. She loved to eat banana."

I snort. "Kinky."

He holds back a smile. "Shh. I'm rhyming here."

I hold my hands in front of my heart and let out an exaggerated breathy sigh.

"One night, she went to see her nanna, who lived in Indiana."

"That's really good," I interrupt in surprise. There's really only so many things that rhyme with Atlanta.

He holds his arms out. "She traveled in a boat, except it didn't float."

"Sad. Terrible luck."

He ignores my interruption and keeps going, talking loudly to the stars and the moon. He's really getting into it.

"So she fell in the water, and said, 'What a bother.' The light was dim, but she landed on Jim..."

I look up at him, waiting for the grand finale.

"And?"

"Jim said, marry me, each night we'll go for a swim, and anytime you have the whim, you're welcome to have some..."

"Banana?" I ask.

"Don't be a pervert," he says.

I laugh. Ridiculous. "What then?"

"You're welcome to have some..." He looks up at the sky, completely stumped. "Okay fine. Banana."

I laugh.

He's so ridiculous. I reach down and splash the cold lake water at him. It splashes across his scarecrow flannel shirt and his face. He sputters, and the look on his face is so shocked and so funny that I can't help but laugh even harder.

The stunned look on his face passes. "You think that's funny?" he asks.

"Mhmm," I say.

He reaches down and splashes a wave of water toward me. I squeal and try to scramble back but the water hits me. I sent a measly amount of water at him, but he hit me with so much that my shirt is drenched.

"Oh, it's on," I say.

Then I reach down and fling as much ice-cold water at him as I can.

I'm laughing and flinging water, and Nathaniel is shoveling handfuls of water back at me.

Pretty soon, we're both drenched and I'm laughing like a loon. The boat is rocking precariously, and I'm slipping around the wet bottom.

I grab onto Nathaniel so I don't fall out. His hair is soaked, his flannel is dripping, and his skin is wet and slippery. I grin up at him and then I notice something I missed over my laughter.

He's laughing too.

It's low and rich, the warmest, happiest sound. It reminds

me of a toasty fireplace in winter that you just want to cozy up to and let it heat you up.

I stop laughing and tilt my chin up so I can watch him. After a second, he stops and looks down at me.

He quirks an eyebrow. "What?" His lips turn up at the corners.

I grip his forearms tighter, to steady myself. "You're..." I trail off.

I look up into his dark eyes. This isn't at all what I had in mind for Romance 101.

It's not...

His eyes move to my lips.

I make a small sound and then reflexively lick my bottom lip. He watches my mouth and something shifts in his expression.

I sway toward him.

His Adam's apple bobs as he swallows.

The night goes still, as if even the stars are holding their breath.

"What now?" he asks.

Next, in the natural order of things, would come the kiss.

That's what happens in Romance 101.

It's slow, languorous, night-scented, and sweet. The kind of kiss you never forget.

My chest clenches painfully.

"Izzy?" he asks. "What's next?"

I beam up at him. "This."

I push my hands against his chest and send him overboard.

His arms pinwheel, his legs hit the edge of the rowboat and he flips into the cold mountain water.

He hits with a splash and water sloshes over the edge of the boat. I grin and lean down. Nathaniel comes up sputtering. His hair is plastered to his forehead and his expression is shocked. He swipes the water off his face.

"Hi there." I grin down at him. "That's the end of your first lesson."

But there's no time to gloat, because the water isn't as deep as I thought.

He stands up, the water comes up to his chest, he grabs the edge of the boat, yanks it sideways and tips me over. I try to grab the sides to keep from falling over, but the bottom of the boat is too slippery and my hands are too wet. I just roll over the side like a kindergartener doing a somersault.

I yelp and hit the water with a splash.

Oh, it's cold. It's so, so cold.

I come up gasping.

Nathaniel may be able to touch bottom, but I can't. Not if I want to breathe. I start shivering right away. I swipe the water out of my eyes and push back my hair. Nathaniel grins at me.

"How's that for romance?" he asks.

"T-t-terrible." I'm so cold. Plus, it's harder than I thought to swim with clothes and shoes on.

I swim over to him and cling to him like a barnacle on an anchor. He looks at me in surprise. I imagine he wasn't expecting me to wrap my arms and legs around his middle.

"Cold," I say.

He nods. "You look awful. Your lips are already purple."

I press my check against his shoulder. He still has warmth.

"Gee, th-th-thanks. Compliments 101 is next on the list. Very important for romance."

He smiles. "I bet."

Then he lifts me up and boosts me back into the boat like I weigh nothing at all. I shiver. It's autumn, I'm soaked, and the night temperature has dropped.

"I'll swim you back to shore," he says.

He must think that he'll capsize the boat if he climbs in. He positions himself at the back, and starts kicking. In less than two minutes we're back to land. I hop onto the grass and wrap my arms around myself.

Nathaniel shakes off. The water sluices off him and forms a puddle at his feet. He looks down at it then up at me with a self-deprecating expression.

"Sorry. I'd give you my shirt if it weren't soaking wet." He pulls it away from his body, it makes a wet smacking sound.

Aww, how sweet. I smile at him. "Lucky for us, there's a room nearby, a hot shower, and a cozy bed with the Berlin Wall of pillows."

But at the mention of pillows and beds I think about lying next to Nathaniel. Another night hearing his breathing and feeling the heat of him under the covers. A part of me can't wait to climb into bed next to him, even with all those pillows between us, and that scares me.

He wants Gertrude and I want him to have Gertrude. I really, really do.

That's all there is to it.

"We won't sleep tonight," I say.

I hurry up the slope, back toward the side entrance of the resort. Nathaniel's long strides keep up with me easily.

"We won't?" he asks.

An image of what people usually do in a romantic resort when there's no sleeping involved flashes through my mind. I angrily shove it aside.

"Obviously not. The clock's ticking, we don't have a minute to spare. I promised to help you win back Gertrude and that's what I'm going to do."

He sends me a grateful look. "Thank you, in case I didn't say it before, thanks. I hope you get David back too. He'd be lucky to have you back. He's blind if he doesn't see that."

I try to shrug off the heavy weight of his words. "I'll be sure to tell him that."

I turn away from Nathaniel and look back over my shoulder at the moonlit lake.

Thank goodness I'm only spending two days in Nathaniel's company, I know I'm supposed to help him and he's supposed to help me, but I really, really don't want to fall in love.

And that's what this is starting to feel like.

**18**

———

It's time for Compliments 101.

Izzy lounges on the bed, propped against the pile of white pillows.

Luckily, Virginia at the front desk was able to find us both sweatpants and T-shirts at the gift shop. They were delivered while Izzy was warming up in the shower. So, Izzy's lips are no longer tinged purple. Instead her cheeks are pink, her skin is glowing, her blonde hair is drying in a cloud around her face, and she looks warm and happy.

She smacks the white down comforter next to her. "Come on, Nathaniel. Make yourself comfortable. It's gonna be a long night."

The way she says Nathaniel, with her southern accent, makes my name sound like a song. Nuh-thaaan-yul. I've never heard anyone pronounce it like that, and when she says it, it makes me feel like smiling.

Which is strange, really strange.

I shouldn't feel anything at all for Izzy. She makes a terrible first impression, she's trouble, and after this weekend I'll never see her again. Plus, Miss Erma confirmed that Gertrude is my soul mate.

So, I say, "Call me Nate."

Izzy tilts her head, "Nate? I thought you didn't like being called Nate."

"I do now."

"I may as well call you Devon."

I give her a sardonic look. "You know, I think life with you would never get boring."

She sits up straighter and gives me a brilliant smile. "There you go. That compliment wasn't half bad. We don't have as much work to do as I thought. Now pop a squat, my neck is getting sore looking up at you."

She pats the bed again. I try to push aside the hesitation I'm feeling. The problem is that while we were in the boat, I felt something. One minute we were laughing and splashing, and the next, the moonlight hit Izzy's face and glistened on the water drops on her lips, and all I wanted to do was kiss her. In fact, I've never wanted to kiss anyone so badly in my life.

I suppose that means she knows what she's doing.

All her talk about the environment creating romance is correct. And, if that's the case, then that means I would've wanted to kiss anyone in that situation.

So apparently, all I need to do is get Gertrude into the

right environment, and she'll remember why we're so good together.

The problem is, I'm having trouble remembering why we're so good together.

I look down at Izzy. She seems comfy in gray sweatpants and a "Romeo is for lovers" t-shirt. I'm in matching sweatpants and a white "I heart Romeo" t-shirt.

I finally give in to Izzy's invitation and settle on the bed, leaving a good three feet of space between us. Even if it was just the environment that made me want to kiss her, there's no reason to tempt fate.

Izzy doesn't seem to notice my internal struggle. She bounces happily on the bed. "Alrighty, then. Compliments 101." She crosses her legs and then puts on her sensei, wise teacher expression.

"I'm ready," I say.

Izzy taps her finger against her lips and looks over at the gas fireplace.

The flames are blue and orange and they dance behind the glass screen. I turned it on as soon as we got back to help Izzy warm up. She thinks for a few seconds then turns back to me.

"There are certain skills you can use to win a woman. Environment..."

"Right," I say. I glance around the room. "A fireplace, a jacuzzi, billowing curtains, a big bed, all in the most romantic town in America. I guess I know why Raphael chose Romeo."

Izzy nods. "But you can beat him at his own game."

Sounds good.

Izzy continues, "Next is compliments. We're going to work on that." She leans back on the pillows and fluffs her hair. "Give me a compliment."

I stare at her. "What? Right now?"

She lifts her eyebrows. "Yes, right now." She gestures to herself. "Lay it on me."

"Okay."

I look at Izzy. I mean, I really, actually look at her.

I know what she looks like, she's short, bouncy, with blue eyes that tilt up impishly at the corners, a permanently smiling mouth, and wavy unrestrained blonde hair. The way she's always moving, either her hands, or her body or her mind, reminds me of a hummingbird zipping around. Colorful and fast. Always flitting to the next experience or the next pretty flower. Always happy. Untouched by life.

I frown.

"Well?" asks Izzy. "Can't come up with anything? Wow. You need more help than I thought."

I shake my head. That's not it. I just realized that I really haven't ever truly *looked* at Izzy.

Because just now, there was much more in her eyes than fun and improvisation and laughter.

There was sadness too, and longing. It was just there, barely hidden beneath the surface. Now that I've noticed it, I can even see it in the way she holds her shoulders and the way she tilts her jaw down and to the left.

She isn't just a magnet for trouble and chaos, or a woman who flits around the world laughing through each day. I don't know why I thought that before, except that I never took a moment to look.

"Sooo...try this," she says. She puts on a low, gravelly voice. "Izzy, you have the most beautiful eyes. Like twin lakes that I want to dive into and stay in forever."

I laugh, glad to have an excuse to stop studying Izzy. "Is that supposed to be my voice?"

"Of course it is. You have as much gravelly growl in your voice as an avalanche. It's enough to make a girl swoon."

I raise my eyebrows.

"Not me," she says. She wrinkles her nose. "I'm talking about Gertrude. Now repeat after me. 'Izzy, you have the most beautiful eyes.'" She says it again in her terrible rendition of me.

I hold back my smile, and comply. "Izzy. You have the most beautiful eyes."

She smiles, batting her eyelashes. She stares into my eyes and I hold her gaze.

"Good," she whispers. "Now say, 'they're like twin lakes that I want to dive into and stay in forever.'"

I shake my head. "That sounds terrible. The lake was freezing. Can you say hypothermia?"

She picks up a pillow and throws it at me. It thuds against my chest.

"Go on," she says.

I set the pillow aside and she resumes her lovelorn pose. I clear my throat and look back at her blue eyes, surprisingly similar to the color of a mountain lake on a clear, autumn day. So, I agree. "They're like twin lakes I want to dive into and stay in forever."

Her shoulders slump and for a second she looks incredibly lonely, even though she's sitting right next to me.

Apparently, I'm terrible at giving compliments. To be fair, I did sound stilted. I pick up the pillow and toss it at her. It smacks her in the chest.

"Hey." She looks up and the spark is back in her eyes. "What was that for?"

"Let me try again." I don't want her to think that I actually can't give a compliment. Or even that she has nothing about her worthy of compliments. There's plenty actually.

"Alright, go ahead." She widens her eyes and gives me another smile, although it's a little dimmer than before and it looks like she has to make an effort to keep it on her face.

I think about everything I know about her. There's lots to like. I think about the first time we met, on the train, with her scamming lunch out of me. Looking back on it, I find a whole lot of humor in the situation. "You really like to eat," I say happily.

Izzy's chin drops and she gives me a flat stare.

Okay, maybe that wasn't the best compliment to begin with. "No, what I mean is that, you eat food like you live life. With relish and enthusiasm. You concentrate completely on what you're eating and pull as much enjoyment from it as possible. Whether it's an apple or a bowl of chocolate mousse. I admire that, because you live life the same way. You appreciate it more than anyone I've ever met."

Izzy's mouth forms an O of surprise. "Oh, that...that was actually really nice," she says in a surprised voice.

Heat prickles on my skin. I'm embarrassed by her appreciation. I look away from her toward the fireplace and the blue and orange flames. There's a picture above the mantle, a couple in a rowboat on the lake. I didn't notice it before.

While I'm turned away, Izzy climbs under the comforter. Then she says, "You did pretty well. There are things about compliments to remember. They should always be genuine and sincere, they should be specific, and they should be given without expecting anything in return. You're giving them solely because you want the woman you are with to feel happy and beautiful."

"Right. Got it," I say. "Let me keep practicing."

"Absolutely. You should practice giving compliments at least three times a day. Preferably for the rest of your life." She smiles and winks at me.

I stare at her a moment. Completely stunned. What would it be like to give her compliments every day for the rest of our lives?

I don't know. But at least I can give some now.

What else do I know about Izzy? She loves food, she's trouble...except, maybe not. Maybe it's not trouble, but adventure.

"I like your sense of adventure," I say. "I think, if I were more like you, I'd live my life differently. You're inspiring."

"Really?" Izzy leans forward and I try to avoid looking the collar of her t-shirt dipping low. "What would you do differently?"

I swallow and look down at my hands resting on my knees. "I wouldn't play life so safe. You were right when we first met, I've been following a route I laid out years ago, but I'm not sure...I don't think it's the right one."

"How so?"

I shrug. "I haven't gotten that far yet. This is my first 'vacation' in ten years. My first time to really think outside of what I have to do at work that day, or what I need to do to make Gertrude happy. Or how to make partner, or buy a bigger home, or get married or..."

"Do you still want Gertrude?"

I was dreading that she'd ask that. "Of course I do." I'm supposed to want her, aren't I? Just like I'm supposed to want partnership and a bigger home and everything else in my life plan.

"Well..." Izzy pauses and smooths out the comforter over her legs. "That's good."

I nod. It is good.

"Then after you and Gertrude get married you can figure out what else you want to do with your life." She looks up at me. "As to everything else, just because you started down a path doesn't mean you can't choose another. There are plenty of doors to open in life. That's half the fun of it."

"I guess you're right," I say.

She nods. "Of course I am."

We smile at each other. A warmth glows in my chest. I decide that the feeling is just the Izzy effect. There's nothing to it beyond that. Izzy is the first to look away.

"So, I think you should practice compliments for Gertrude."

I nod. "I was thinking the same thing."

"What do you usually compliment her on?"

I'm getting sore sitting cross-legged on the cushy bed, so I move up to the pillows and lean on them next to Izzy. She scoots closer to me.

"Well?"

I think back over the last three years. "I compliment her on how nice she looks. She likes to wear jeweled brooches, so I compliment her when she finds a new one."

"Okay. Serious question here," Izzy says.

I nod.

"Are you absolutely certain Gertrude's not actually an eighty-year-old woman with a really good plastic surgeon?"

I'm tempted to throw another pillow at Izzy but I restrain myself. "I'm sure."

"Alright. Fine. What else?" asks Izzy.

I lean into the plush pillows and think back. "I compliment her on how hard she works at her job. She's a senior accountant, and she's extremely dedicated."

"Hmm. And she likes it when you compliment her?"

I shake my head. "I don't know. Usually she brushes it aside."

"Uh huh."

"What? I'm always sincere, specific...what was the other?" I look over at Izzy. She's sunk into the pillows and has rolled even closer to me. I don't bother scooting away.

"Giving without expecting anything in return? Did you except something in return?"

I think about it. "Not really." Although... "Maybe. Maybe I expected her love."

I look across the room at the sheer curtains and the window looking over the dark lake. Stupidly, I'm embarrassed to have said that out loud. It just popped into my head. I turn back to Izzy, irritated at how she gets me to say things that probably aren't even true.

"Never mind," I say. "I don't think that was true."

I'm going to say more, but I don't because Izzy is giving me a smile I haven't seen before. She reaches out and puts her hand on my arm. She's warm, and the feel of her spreads through me.

"Do you know the worst thing about expecting?" she asks in a quiet voice.

My throat aches, so I swallow and try to clear it. "What?" I ask, although I think I know.

"Expecting always leads to disappointment."

The room suddenly feels too small, the air too hot.

"Don't expect," she says. "Izzy's number one rule for life. Don't expect. That way, people can't disappoint you, they can only pleasantly surprise you. Situations can't hurt you, they can only be what they are. Life just is. Don't expect."

Her voice is thick.

I look down at her hand on my arm. She's trying to reassure me, but instead, all her touch is doing is sending a warm, haze through my blood. It's hard to think.

"Are you talking from experience?" I ask.

I'm trying to distract myself from the image I have of taking Izzy's hand in mine, flipping her beneath me, pressing into her, and kissing her senseless. Without any expectations. None. No expectations.

"Of course I am," Izzy says.

I shake my head. What were we talking about?

"I only give advice based on experience."

Oh. Right.

I glance up from her hand and look at her mouth. It's cherry red, and the corners curve up.

"Did you know, you have a freckle that looks just like a heart above your mouth?" I ask. "I never noticed that before." I start to reach up to touch it.

When I do, Izzy freezes for a moment.

Then, right before I reach her, she scrambles off the bed.

She's off of the bed so fast that pillows fall to the floor after her. She stands a few feet away from me, eyes wide, expression shocked.

What the heck just happened?

We stare at each other, neither of us speaking.

Izzy pulls in quick breaths. Her cheeks are flushed.

"That's enough..." she starts, then, "you're all good on compliments."

I frown. "I'm sorry. I didn't mean to imply anything." I shake my head. Things are confusing. This is confusing. "I want Gertrude," I clarify, probably more for me than Izzy.

She rubs her hands down her sweatpants and nods. "I know. I just...need to use the bathroom."

I close my eyes as she hurries to the bathroom and shuts the door. I smack my head against the headboard. Idiot. Idiot.

What was I thinking?

I open my eyes.

There's the fire. The sheer curtains, the wine, the cozy bed. I wasn't thinking. That's just it. This room is a romantic environment. Once again, I was trapped by Izzy's first rule of romance. Of course.

I climb out of the bed and sit on the desk chair.

There. Much better.

I hear the faucet running in the bathroom and some

splashing. When Izzy comes out, I'll be cool and collected and ready for my next lesson.

I look at the clock. It's two in the morning. Only four or five more hours before Izzy and I can leave, and I can start pursuing Gertrude again.

No problem. I'm sure I won't be tempted to touch Izzy again. Especially now that I know it was the romantic environment influencing me.

No touching. No problem.

I pick up the bottle of local wine and decide to uncork it. That might help me relax. I pour the wine and smell notes of blackberry jam and oak. I take a drink. Delicious.

I glance up when Izzy comes out of the bathroom. It looks like she splashed her cheeks with cold water. She has a determined expression on her face.

"Alrighty," she says in a no-nonsense voice. "Next lesson."

"Okay. What is it?" I take another drink of the wine.

"I'm going to teach you how to touch a woman."

Instead of swallowing, I spray the wine across the carpet and over the white comforter.

"It's that good?" Izzy asks with a smirk.

No touching? No problem?

What a disaster.

# 19

---



Nathaniel

Izzy sits cross-legged on the bed.

We're positioned face to face and sitting so close that I can smell the lavender shampoo she used earlier this evening in the shower. I try to relax my shoulders, but I can't. In fact, my whole body is tense.

"You need to relax," Izzy smirks and shakes her head at me. There's a load of humor in her eyes.

"I am relaxed." I roll my shoulders and slump a bit into the cushy bed. "See?"

She scoffs. "Ha. You're about as relaxed as a virgin in a medieval romance about to be ravished by her muscle-bound warrior lord."

I picture this cowering virgin and her bulky lord. "I don't think so."

Izzy goes to set her hand on my arm and I stiffen. She sends me a pointed look.

I lean forward. "Look. This is one lesson that I don't need. Like I said, Gertrude and I are compatible in this department."

Izzy eyes darken and she scowls at me. I get the feeling I just flunked this part of her lesson.

"So, you're not talking about sex?" I ask.

She smacks her head with her hand. "Of course I'm not talking about sex." She pins me with an exasperated look. "I'm talking about wooing a woman. Romance. Do you think Raphael stole Gertrude with sex?"

"You said—"

"Sure. They're going at it like rabbits in springtime."

I flinch at the description.

"Sorry." She pats my arm. "But, trust me, Raphael didn't substitute a handshake with sex upon first meeting Gertrude. Instead, he used the power of touch."

I try to wrap my head around this. "Okay. Touch."

She nods. "Touch."

She bites her lip and looks up at the ceiling, apparently thinking through how she wants to proceed. Finally, she drops her chin and smiles at me.

I lift an eyebrow. "Got it?"

"Sure do."

She reaches out and grabs my hands.

I hold still, waiting for some magical spark to overwhelm me. I frown down at her fingers holding mine. She's colder than I am, her hands are soft and delicate, but beyond that the only thing I feel is a bit of happiness lodged in my chest.

"Am I supposed to feel something?" I ask.

She snorts and I look up to see her laughing at me. "No. I'm demonstrating. How often do you hold Gertrude's hand?"

I shake my head. "Gertrude doesn't like holding hands, she says it's childish and pedestrian."

"Huh. Okay. Hmm."

I think that for the first time in her life, Izzy is speechless. I'd laugh if she weren't speechless at my expense.

"Anyway," she says, pulling herself back together. "Touch is a language. When you hold hands with someone, you're saying, 'I like you, we're together, we're comfortable.' See?" She nods down to our hands. I look at her fingers covering my hand.

I guess I see that. "Okay?"

"Now try this. When we entwine our fingers, we're saying 'we're linked, we're combined, I'm a part of you and you're a part of me.' Go ahead." She squeezes my hand.

I look into her eyes and she gives an encouraging nod. I draw in a slow breath and then thread my fingers with hers. She was right. My palm presses against hers, there's warmth and awareness and I feel more connected to her. The pulse in my wrist picks up and my hand tingles.

"Feel that?" she whispers.

I give a slow nod.

She smiles with satisfaction then pulls her hand from mine. The tingling warmth fades and leaves behind cold. I blink owlishly at her. The light from the fireplace licks over her skin and gives her a golden glow. It's easy to forget how pretty she is. Maybe it's because she rarely sits still. She's usually a blur of color and movement and laughter. When she sits still the rest of her comes into focus.

"Like I said, touch is a language." Izzy folds her hands in her lap. "You can communicate to someone how much you love them, how much you want them, how much you're going to pleasure them through the briefest of touches."

The tingling feeling is starting again. Izzy doesn't need touch, she only needs words and her presence. I wish I'd met her before Gertrude ran off with Raphael. Then she would've taught me...no, no she wouldn't have. I wouldn't have given her a second look when I was with Gertrude. The only reason we're here is because of necessity.

"Do you follow?" Izzy asks.

I give a quick nod. "Touch is a language."

She sends me a sassy grin. "Good. Now, you're going to use touch as romance."

**20**

———————

Nathaniel

Suddenly the room feels hotter. I pull at the collar of my t-shirt. "We're not going to…"

Izzy rolls her eyes. "Of course not. You're not even getting to first base. We're friends, Nate, not lovers."

I stare at her, stunned by her statement. "We're friends?"

She gives a delicate snort. "Of course we are."

I think about this for a minute. Finally I say, "I hadn't thought of that."

She grins. Then she scoots closer until our legs are touching and she's practically in my lap. "Let's get started. Here are the rules. You can only touch my face, shoulders and neck, my arms and hands, and my legs from the knees down. Nowhere else."

I nod. Good rules. Nice, platonic rules. "Sounds good."

"I'm going to touch you first, and then you mimic my touch. After you get the hang of it, you can try touches on your own. Okay?"

My mouth goes dry. "Right." My voice comes out gravelly, so I clear my throat. "Right."

Izzy reaches forward. I think she's going to touch my arm, or my shoulder, but instead her fingers drift up and draw along the side of my face, brush over the hair at my temple, and then run featherlight down my jaw. I hold back a shiver. Even after she lifts her fingers I can still feel the whisper of her on my skin.

"Now you," she says.

The fire crackles behind her, and the down-filled comforter shifts beneath me as I lean forward. I focus on the dip where her temple meets her glossy hair. Finally I touch just the barest tip of my fingers to her skin. She's softer than I thought she'd be, and warmer. I drift my hands over to her hair. It glistens like gold in the orange glow of the room. The waves of her hair feel like silk and they slip through my fingers. I move my fingers back to her cheek and draw them down her jaw. Her cheeks flush rosy pink. I want to touch her lips to see if they feel as lush as they look. But I don't. I mimic what she did and slowly lift my hand from the edge of her jaw.

My body is tense. "How was that?" I ask. My voice is gravelly again. I ignore it.

"Good," she says and I'm satisfied that she sounds breathy. "Now try this."

I watch as her tongue darts out and wets her bottom lip. I'm so focused on the glossy sheen of her mouth that I miss it when she sets her fingers to the underside of my knee. Even through my sweatpants, I can feel her. No one has ever touched me there before. It feels good.

Better than good.

"There are places on the body more sensitive than others," Izzy says in an instructive voice.

But I'm having a hard time listening, because she's dragging her hand down my leg and then back up it to play under my knee again.

She continues, "there's the underside of the knee. The ankles. The wrists. The neck. The ears. Plenty more. You just have to find them."

My head is muzzy and dazed. Probably because it's nearly three o'clock in the morning. Probably.

"Now you," Izzy says.

I nod. If I didn't know better, I'd think that I'd drunk the entire bottle of wine and not just a few sips. I explore Izzy's knee, her calf, her ankle, and then I move back up. The blood is quickly leaving my head.

Touch works. Touch definitely works.

"One more," Izzy says.

She moves to her knees and leans closer to me. Her hair falls around her face and sends the delicate scent of lavender to me. Her T-shirt is baggy and the collar opens so that if I looked down I'd be able to see the flushed skin of her chest. More.

She's dressed in oversized sweatpants and a touristy T-shirt. Even though she should look ridiculous, she doesn't. She looks like a siren.

She reaches up with both hands and places them gently

on my cheeks. Her fingertips drift over my eyebrows, I close my eyes as she gently runs the pads of her fingers over my eyelids, then she lets one hand run down my neck to rest over my throbbing pulse, while the thumb of her other hand pulls my lower lip down. I keep my eyes closed as she explores my mouth with her thumb and her fingers. Her other hand plays at the base of my throat.

"This touch is prelude to a kiss," she says.

My eyes snap open. She slowly pulls her thumb from my lip and her fingers from my neck. The air around us feels as thick and sweet as honey. Almost like the sound of Izzy's voice. It's hard to breathe in it.

I reach for the remote for the fireplace and turn the setting to low.

Izzy looks at me questioningly.

"It's hot in here," I say gruffly.

Izzy grins then fans herself. "Hubba hubba. But Compliments 101 is over." She gestures to herself. "Your turn. Remember, it's a language. A prelude. A promise. Try to make me feel what you want Gertrude to feel. Tomorrow, you'll see her, speak to her, touch her. I want you to be ready."

She drops back to the bed and closes her eyes. "Lay it on me. Be my Casanova."

She looks so relaxed that I decide to poke the bear. "Are you sure you'll be able to resist me? I mean, I am learning my skills from the best."

She opens one eye to squint at me. "I'll be fine." She closes her eye and then gives an indelicate, jaw-cracking yawn.

I take it as a challenge. But before I start, I ask, "Where'd you learn all this anyway?"

She blows out a breath that ruffles her hair. She doesn't open her eyes. "I had a wonderful fiancé who treated me exceptionally well. He taught me lots about love and romance."

Oh. No wonder she doesn't want to let him go. My head clears a bit and I don't feel as muzzy or overheated.

Izzy waves her hand in the air. "Come on then. Imagine Gertrude."

Right.

I try to imagine Izzy with auburn hair instead of blonde and a straighter nose instead of one that's slightly rounded. I picture her skin paler and I take away the heart-shaped freckle over her mouth. In fact, her mouth is wrong too. I try to imagine it thinner, and firmer like Gertrude's. Plus, Izzy's jaw is soft, while Gertrude's is sharper. Gertrude is beautiful in an angular, modern art sort of way. Izzy is so full of movement that every time I look at her I feel like I'm on the tilt-a-whirl at the fair. I'm spinning dizzily, my heart is pounding and I just want to grab her and hold her tight so I don't lose her while we're propelled around in circles.

I shake my head. It's not working. I can't picture Gertrude. Izzy is too Izzy for this to work.

"Stop smiling," I say. "I'm having a hard time picturing her."

Izzy's brow wrinkles. "Oh." She huffs and her hair shifts around her shoulders again. "How's this?"

She presses her lips into a firm, straight line.

"Ummm. Not quite."

She sniffs, then pulls her eyebrows down to form a little worry line between them. "This?"

I hold back a smile. She doesn't look more like Gertrude, she just looks like Izzy with a frown. Which looks all wrong.

"Maybe try sticking your chin out. Like you're running a business meeting," I suggest.

"Oooh. Why didn't you say so? I'm running a meeting. Got it."

I shake my head at her. She's so ridiculous.

The tip of her tongue goes to the edge of her mouth while she thinks. I don't think she's going to be able to pull it off, but suddenly she transforms.

She goes from soft, dizzy-making motion to...well, another person. She sits up straight on the bed, her jaw sticks out, her eyebrows pull down, and her mouth goes firm. She's hard-edged and serious. Humorless. I don't recognize anything about her. It's almost as if she's put on a business suit, a pair of glasses and traded her backpack for a briefcase. I almost expect that any second she'll start talking about profits and losses.

"Izzy?" I ask, which is stupid, because I know it's her.

"Hurry up, Nate. Do the thing." She waves her hands again for me to proceed. At least that's the same.

I take a breath. I still can't picture Gertrude, but I have another need. To clear this look from Izzy's face and make her go back to her old self. The smiling, mischief-making Izzy.

I reach up with both my hands and cup her face. Her mouth softens a bit, but the rest of her stays stern and humorless. I run my thumbs over the arch of her eyebrows and smooth out the wrinkle between her brow.

Then I run my fingertips over her eyelids and down her cheeks. I feel her softening beneath me. I take my thumb to her mouth. It's still a hard, firm line, so I tug on it and play with the lush softness of it. I rub my thumb in the wetness of her inner lip and then rub it over her mouth, drawing away the hardness. I study every minute movement, every intake of breath, the slope of her shoulders. Each time I move my fingers across her skin I watch her reaction, if she relaxes into me, I do more of what I was doing. I trail my free hand down her neck and find her pulse. It's beating quickly. I circle my fingers over it, then move to the little indented vee at the bottom of her throat. I drag my fingers across the vee and she gives a little, involuntary sound.

Her eyes fly open.

We stare at each other.

Her cheeks are flushed pink. Her pulse is quick and her breathing fast. She's back to herself again, but not. Because although her lips are curved up, and her eyes are bright, there's also a vulnerability and a longing in her expression.

I'm dizzy again, like we're spinning, and I want to drag her into my arms.

I draw her lip between my thumb and forefinger and gently pull on it. She makes another small noise. Her eyes widen.

This is when we kiss. The thought pops into my mind. Touch is a prelude. This is when we kiss.

I move my hands to the back of Izzy's head and wrap my

fingers in her hair. Her pupils dilate and her eyes turn a deeper, darker blue.

The bedding rustles beneath us, a soft whisper of fabric. Izzy's hair feels like corn silk in my hands. I wonder what she tastes like? If she tastes like she feels. Soft and dizzy-making and honey sweet.

I pull her close, until our mouths are only an inch apart and all she has to do is move forward, just an inch. It'd be as easy as breathing.

I look into her eyes. There are gray flecks in the blue that I never noticed before. I rub my fingers through her hair.

"Izzy?" I whisper. "What are we doing?"

She tilts her head and I run my fingers over her skin. I see the shift in her expression. She forces back the vulnerability and the longing and replaces it with humor.

"Touching lessons," she says. She hasn't pulled back. So I do. We aren't meant to kiss. That wouldn't be right. I untangle my hands from her hair and scoot back.

"Are we done? Did I pass?"

Izzy straightens her t-shirt and sweatpants. "Obviously," she says nonchalantly, but she doesn't look at me.

I frown and glance around the room. The fire glows in the dim light. The sheer curtains sway from the breeze of the heater. Our dinner tray is on the desk, one half of a croissant is all that remains. The bed Izzy and I lounge on is plush and comfortable. The entire scene is intimate.

I frown at the room then take in Izzy fidgeting with the drawstring of her sweatpants.

Maybe we shouldn't do this anymore. It feels like we're quickly approaching a boundary that shouldn't be crossed.

Gertrude may be mating like a rabbit with Raphael, but I still consider myself in a relationship. We're soul mates. We're meant to be. I'm taken. And Izzy's taken too.

"You love David, right?" I ask.

Izzy stiffens, she looks up and her eyes shift lightning fast from warm blue to ice.

"What?" I don't understand the change in her demeanor. "What's wrong?"

She shakes her head angrily. "Of course I love him. Why do you think I'm here? Doing this?" She forcefully gestures at me then at herself.

I raise my eyebrows. "For David?"

"Exactly," she says. "And for me."

Warning flags go up and a sick feeling settles in my stomach. "Are you using me to make him jealous?"

She looks at me like I'm crazy. "No."

"Or am I a rebound lay? Is that what you're aiming for?"

Her face loses all color and suddenly I feel like a jerk.

"Izzy, I didn't mean it. I know you want him back…" I trail off when I see the vulnerability and hurt in her expression. "I didn't mean it. I know you're trying to help. I just don't get why."

She stares at me challengingly, but the vulnerability is still there. "Maybe I don't understand why I'm helping you either. Did you ever think about that? Maybe it just felt like fate. How's that? Is that good enough?"

I consider this. "Good enough," I finally agree. "We'll call it fate."

Her shoulders relax and she lets out a long breath. "Maybe we could sleep a bit after all?" she asks. "I'm kind of tired." She piles the pillows into a high wall in the center of the bed.

"Good idea." I help stack the pillows up into a two-foot-tall, two-foot-wide tower. When we're done I reach over and flip off the desk light. The clock says four in the morning.

I hear the rustle of sheets as she settles under the blanket. I lie on top of the comforter. I fold my arms under my head, look up at the ceiling and let out a long sigh. The fireplace casts shadows and a slight orange glow over the room.

"Don't worry, Nathaniel," Izzy says sleepily.

"Why's that?" I ask. I turn my head but I can't see Izzy over the tower of pillows.

"'Cause, Gertrude will be back in your arms by tomorrow."

"And Izzy will be gone" remains unsaid.

I look back up at the ceiling. There's a hollow ache in my chest that persists long after Izzy's breathing evens out and she falls asleep. It even persists into my dreams.

# 21

Izzy

"I think coffee is the best thing in the world," I say.

I take a long sip of my hazelnut latte and study Nathaniel over the brim of my mug.

His eyes have dark smudges under them and he keeps yawning. I'd bet my last dollar that he didn't sleep a bit.

When I woke up at eight, Nathaniel was already shaved and showered and raring to head to downtown Romeo to buy some new clothes. Not that he doesn't look adorable in his sweats and "I heart Romeo" t-shirt.

In fact, I really like how the pants hang low over his hips and the t-shirt is slightly too small and molds his chest and shoulders perfectly. I like him in casual wear. Although, I liked him in a suit as well. I mentally shrug, I guess I like him in everything.

"You don't mean that," Nathaniel says. He takes a long swallow of his red eye, a black coffee with two shots of espresso.

"Mean what?"

His lips curl up and I'm happy to see that he's smiling.

"That coffee is the best thing in the world," he says.

Downtown Romeo is framed behind him. We're sitting at an outdoor café table at The SweetStop, an adorable bakery on Main Street. It's not quite nine o'clock. We're waiting for the little clothing boutique to open so that Nathaniel can find an outfit that shows off his best assets.

"What do I think is the best thing then?" I ask.

I smile back at him and take another long sip of my coffee. It's hot and smooth and has the perfect note of hazelnut. It reminds me of sitting outside a bakery in Geneva, Switzerland the smell of toasted hazelnuts and chocolate in the air.

"Isn't it obvious?" he says with a knowing smirk. He holds out his hand in front of himself.

For a second, I think he's implying that I like him best of all in the world. I go to protest, but something stops me, because I do like him.

I like him a lot.

I look at his smile, his dark eyes and the stubble that grows on his jaw barely two hours after shaving. There's a yearning in me that wants to agree with him, but then it's snatched away. I can't. Then I look to where he's actually gesturing and realize that he's pointing to my plate of Nutella croissants.

"Ahh," I say thickly, "you're right. I do like croissants better than coffee."

He winks, then reaches down and steals one of my croissants. When he takes a bite the pastry flakes down and falls to the table like snow. When he tastes the buttery meltiness of the croissant his eyes widen and he chews more vigorously.

"Mmm, that's good," he says, his mouth still full. His eyes widen. "That's really good. What've I been missing all these years?"

I stifle a laugh. "Stick with me. I'll show you all the wonders of the universe."

He stuffs the last of the croissant into his mouth and chews happily. His egg white and spinach omelet is only half-finished. Apparently, I've turned him to the dark side.

I flake off some pastry from the edge of a croissant and nibble at it.

He wipes his mouth with his napkin and then gives me a satisfied smile.

I ignore the pinching sensation in my chest.

"Have you always smiled this much?" I ask. "Because, to be honest, when we first met, you looked like you hadn't smiled in years. Like, Oscar the Grouch territory."

He lifts his eyebrow, but the smile stays on his lips. "Really? That bad?"

I try to clarify. "I mean, I know you were having a bad day. So I was just wondering, is this your regular expression?" I gesture at him, at the cute little smile on his face and the amusement in his eyes. "Or are you usually like you were on the train? All Mr. Serious," I say in a lower voice.

He snorts and then takes a long sip of his coffee. Then, when he sets it on the table, he says, "I don't have a mirror handy to check my expression minute by minute, but…"

"But?"

He gives me a sly look and then grabs the last croissant.

"Hey," I say in protest. "That had my name on it."

"Sure it did," he says. Then I watch as he delicately tears the croissant in two. Little pastry flakes twirl to the table, and the fragrance of Nutella fills the air. My mouth waters as he holds half out to me. He watches me with a glint in his eyes.

"Izzy's half," he says. I open my hand and he drops the warm croissant onto my palm.

"Nathaniel's half," he says, holding up his piece.

I can't help but smile at him.

He taps his croissant to mine and then takes a happy bite. The Nutella runs down my fingers, so I shove the croissant into my mouth and chew. Then I lick the Nutella off. So, so good.

When Nathaniel has finished every last crumb he says, "To answer your question, you're right. I haven't smiled as much as I have since I met you, in…years." He looks thoughtful for a moment then says more seriously, "It's been years."

"I'm sorry," I say. I reach out and put my hand on his arm.

He looks down at my hand resting on the warm skin of his forearm, then he smiles at me.

"Nathaniel Barry, my Aunt Erma told me you were in town!"

I snatch my hand from Nathaniel's arm and look past him. There's a cute, young woman in a poufy floral dress, beaming at Nathaniel.

"Chloe?" asks Nathaniel, like he's not quite sure.

Chloe nods, "that's me. Wow. I haven't seen you since we were fighting over the swings at that playground in New York. Remember that?"

Nathaniel looks back at me and gives me a sardonic look, as if to say, "Who me? I'd never fight over swings."

I'd enjoy the idea, except I'm grappling with the weirdest sensation. It feels almost like jealousy, which is crazy, because I'm actively trying to help Nathaniel woo another woman. So that can't be right.

Chloe moves next to the table. She's set down a sketchbook and is showing Nathaniel some drawings.

"I'm doing this card line on soul mates. It was Veronica's idea. She's my business partner. My aunt told you about our greeting card company, right?"

Nathaniel nods, and even though he's wearing a tee and sweats, he looks business-like and serious again. "She mentions it almost every time we talk. That and your baby."

Chloe blushes a pretty shade of pink and gives the sort of smile that you see on moms that love their kids wholeheartedly.

Then Chloe seems to realize that Nathaniel isn't alone. She looks at me and her eyes widen. "Oh I'm sorry. I got carried away. I always do when I'm talking about new card ideas. And then I was thinking about swings and my aunt and you must be Nathaniel's soul mate. My aunt told me all about how she saw you and you'd be in town this weekend and how you're just perfect for Nathaniel." Chloe holds out her hand for me to shake and gives me a big, happy smile. "I'm Chloe by the way. It's so nice meeting you."

I stare at her hand. Nathaniel has gone stiff and completely still. His face is totally devoid of expression. Awkward. This is so awkward.

I clear my throat. "Oh. I'm not..." I shake my head, "I'm not Nathaniel's soul mate. I'm...helping him get his soul mate back. Errr...I'm...Izzy."

Chloe looks confused, then embarrassed. She wrinkles her nose and then shakes her head. "I'm sorry. I just assumed, you looked so cozy together and happy and I thought..." She tilts her head and studies us. Nathaniel has relaxed a bit. He's looking between Chloe and me.

"We just met Thursday. On the train," he explains. Then, more firmly, "We're just friends."

I take Chloe's hand. She has paint and ink on her fingertips, and there are little callouses, I'm assuming from where she holds her pens and paintbrushes. She gives me a warm, self-deprecating smile and shakes my hand. I realize that I like her, I really like her.

"Nice to meet you, Izzy," she says as she pumps my hand.

"Likewise," I say.

Chloe picks up her sketchbook and holds it to her chest. "Well, my studio is just up there." She points to the windows above the bakery. "If you need anything, let me know." She turns to Nathaniel, "I hope everything works out. Trust me, I know how crazy things can get when it comes to soul mates. I hope you find everything you're looking for."

"He will," I tell her confidently. "I'm helping him. Nothing can go wrong."

Nathaniel snorts into his coffee. I kick him under the table. I'm sure he's thinking about all the things that have already gone wrong, but that was the past and this is today.

Chloe nods, "I'm sure it'll work out great. Erma's predictions always come true."

"Exactly," Nathaniel says.

I wonder why he doesn't sound as excited as I thought he would. Shouldn't he be happy that it's practically guaranteed he'll get Gertrude back?

After Chloe leaves we finish our coffee, Nathaniel puts money on the table for the bill.

"I'll pay you back," I tell him as we walk toward the little boutique.

"It's nothing," he says.

Apparently, he has no idea that when your bank account is empty and you don't have a home, a meal is a lot more than nothing.

**22**

———

SHOPPING WAS A SUCCESS. OOH LA LA, THE ONLY CLOTHING boutique in town, had a small men's section, but there was enough choice to make it work.

"You look good," I tell Nathaniel.

He actually looks better than good. He's in a new pair of leather shoes, dark form-fitting jeans, a tight long-sleeve Henley, a sexy jacket and aviator sunglasses. This outfit was just about the only option in the store, but it works on him.

"Gertrude won't be able to keep her hands off you," I tell him.

He lowers his sunglasses and gives me a practiced look.

"Hubba hubba," I say. I fan myself and he grins at my reaction.

We're walking down Main Street, back up to the country

road that leads to the resort. It's a short walk, less than two miles, and I'm sure Nathaniel wants to get back, but there's something I need to do before we leave town.

I take a deep breath of the crisp, autumn-leaf-scented air.

"I have another lesson before we head back," I say.

Nathaniel stops and puts his hands in his pockets. "Really? In town?"

"Mmmhmm." I nod at the chocolate shop. "Gift giving."

Even though the sunglasses are hiding his expression I can tell that the corners of Nathaniel's eyes are crinkling in humor. "I give gifts."

I flush. Nathaniel noticed how cold I've been in the autumn weather, so he threw a pair of jeans, a long cashmere sweater and a knitted scarf at me in the boutique. "Put these on," he said in a "don't argue with me, Izzy" sort of voice.

I'd asked if accepting clothes from him meant I was his mistress now and if he expected some hot virgin sex in exchange. He just rolled his eyes and said it only meant that he was sick of giving me his wet shirts when I was shivering.

I smile at Nathaniel and rub my hand across the soft cashmere of my sweater. It was a really, really nice gift.

"True. But we're talking about romance here," I clarify. "Romantic gifts."

He combs his fingers through his hair and I can't help but think that he looks like a different person. A relaxed, happy person.

"Alright," he says. "What sort of gifts should I be giving Gertrude? Jewelry? Flowers?"

I bite my lip. The more I'm with Nathaniel, the less I feel

like I'm doing the right thing. In fact, doing the right thing feels like doing the wrong thing. Helping him get back with Gertrude feels wrong. I wince when I realize that I've bitten my lip so hard it's bleeding.

It doesn't matter. Last night when he asked if I was using him, he was right. In a way, I am using him. But if using him sends him back to Gertrude, well, that's what he wants, isn't it? And if it means sending me onward, able to move on, well, that's what I want too, isn't it?

So, if doing the right thing feels wrong, then so be it.

I nod at Nathaniel. "Jewelry and flowers are good. But I'm going to teach you something better."

He gives me a skeptical look, like you can't surpass the ultimate gifting of jewelry and flowers.

I gesture at the chocolate shop across the street. There are rows of chocolates displayed in the window, and even across the street I can smell the scent of melted chocolate, sugar and spice.

"Here's what you do, go across the street to the chocolate shop and get a dozen chocolates. Get their 'I Love You' heart box. Okay?"

"Alright." He studies the cute little shop. My heart gives a tight, hard thud against my rib cage. I don't want to do this anymore. Not really. But c'est la vie.

"I'll be sitting on that bench by the river." I point to a little wooden bench next to the Romeo River.

It's situated under an oak tree with deep red and flaming orange leaves. The bench overlooks a small arched bridge that spans the river.

"When you have the box of chocolates, come over, get down on one knee and hold the chocolates out to me and say, "a sweet for my sweet." Open the lid and offer one." I look away from the bench and back to Nathaniel. "That's how you give a romantic gift," I clarify.

He quirks an eyebrow. "A sweet for my sweet? Cheesy works?"

I shrug.

"Do I get to eat them too? Or are they only for you?" he asks.

The tightness in my chest bursts, and I shove at him. "Go on. I'll be waiting."

I wander down the block until I come to the little park at the river's edge. The morning has turned into a blue sky day, and the fall leaves are brilliant against the blue backdrop. I sit down on the bench, look at the flowing river, and wrap my arms around myself. The hard wooden bench digs into my thighs and the cold of the wood seeps through my jeans. The bench is in the shade of the tree. The sweater's warm, but I still feel a chill. I shiver and hold myself tighter.

Maybe this wasn't a good idea.

No, there's no maybe about it. This wasn't a good idea at all. I can't keep doing this to myself. I really can't.

I kick at the dirt beneath the bench and scowl at the ants crawling by. The smell of earth rises to me, dirt and soil and decomposing leaves. My throat tightens and a I feel tears at the back of my eyes. I hate the smell of dirt. I hate...

"A sweet for my sweet," Nathaniel says.

I look up in surprise. Nathaniel is down on one knee,

only a few feet away, holding out a heart box full of chocolates.

My heart thuds. What am I doing? What am I doing?

He's on one knee. He's smiling at me. He has a box of 'I Love You' chocolates.

What am I doing?

Nathaniel looks at my expression and then scowls. "I knew the cheesy saying wouldn't work. Look at you, you look like you're about to be sick. How about this?" He thrusts the chocolates forward. "Chocolates are sweet and so are you..." He quirks an eyebrow at me.

The tightness in my throat vanishes. "Go on," I say, and I'm glad to find that my voice is steady.

He narrows his eyes in thought. "Chocolates are sweet and so are you...let's eat the whole box, yum, yum, chew." He gives me a triumphant grin. I hold back a laugh.

"How was that?" he asks.

"Terrible, really, truly—" I cut off.

There on the bridge a couple walks hand in hand toward us. They're only thirty feet away. My eyes widen. I'd recognize that auburn-haired woman and blond stud anywhere.

It's Gertrude and Raphael.

They pause to lean on the railing of the bridge and look down into the water. Raphael kisses Gertrude's shoulder.

I look from them to Nathaniel.

I'm not ready for him to confront her yet. No wait, that's backwards. He's not ready to confront her yet. It has to be a time of his choosing. When he has the advantage.

Right. There's only one thing to do.

"What is it?" asks Nathaniel.

He's still smiling at me. He has no idea his almost-fiancée is behind him canoodling with her lover.

Raphael and Gertrude walk toward us again. They'll see us any minute. Maybe Gertrude will recognize Nathaniel. Even in his new clothes, he's hard to mistake for anyone else, he has too much presence, too much...Nathaniel.

They make it to the edge of the bridge. Gertrude turns our way.

Decision made.

I spring off the bench and launch myself onto Nathaniel. The box of chocolates falls to the ground, flies open, and chocolates spill everywhere.

Nathaniel loses his balances, he slips in the grass, and falls backwards. I land on top of him with a jarring thud. He's hard, and warm and he smells like Nutella croissant and chocolates. He grips my ribs and looks up at me with a humorous but unsurprised expression.

"So, you liked the gift?" he asks.

My chest presses to his, I can feel his heart beating steadily beneath mine. My legs wrap around his middle. I look toward the bridge, Gertrude and Raphael have stopped walking and are staring at us.

Nathaniel runs his hands over my back. "Umm, Izzy?" he says.

Crap. Crappity crap.

"Gertrude and Raphael are here," I whisper.

"What?" He moves like he's going to look around, or get up.

"Shhh." I lean closer and touch my nose to his. "Pretend we're in love."

He gives me a dumbfounded look. "If they recognize me from the café, they'll assume you're Devon, my French-tickling husband. You're super horny. Yeah?"

His cheeks turn pink and suddenly I become aware that I'm straddling Nathaniel in public, his hands are gripping my back, and I'm leaning over him.

"Kiss me," I say.

Nathaniel coughs, then manages, "Excuse me?"

"Do you want to talk to Gertrude when you're in control, at your time and place of choosing, or do you want to talk to her now with Raphael at her side while you're lying in the mud?"

His mouth thins. "Fair point. I choose kissing."

"Pretend it's just another lesson," I say.

He moves one hand down to my sacrum and pulls me closer, then he moves his other hand to my cheek and pulls me down. My long hair forms a curtain between us and the rest of the world. Nathaniel threads his fingers through my hair and tugs me down until my mouth meets his.

It's a gentle touching of our lips, soft, as light as a feather. Even so, at that tiny contact an aching need bursts to life inside me. It's heavy and warm. I let out a small gasp. Nathaniel's eyes are open, watching me, and I see the second he realizes that I'm feeling exactly what he is. Our kiss goes from a gentle touching of lips to more. Much more.

He grips my hair and grinds my mouth against his. I make another noise and he opens his mouth and sends his tongue across my lower lip. I open to him, and let him in. He explores my mouth. I suck on him and taste him. He tastes like my favorite things, coffee, croissants, chocolate, Nathaniel. His hand presses firmly against my back, his fingers dig into me and he rocks my hips against him. I can feel the thickness, the hardness of him, and I want more. I can't think of anything but wanting more.

He bites at my lip and sucks on me.

His hands explore my face, my neck, my back and my hips. This is like his touch from last night, magnified by a thousand.

If last night was a flame, this is an inferno.

I have to touch him, I have to move. I run my hands through his hair, grip it in my hands and position his mouth so I can taste him better. Kiss him more. Then that isn't enough, because he's rocking against me in a way that has cleared my mind of anything but needing him.

Touch is a language, and right now, his hands are firm, and forceful and he's guiding me right into heaven.

He squeezes my hips and rocks me against him again. I give a cry at the spark I feel between my legs. It's throbbing and aching, and I haven't felt this way in so long that I'm mindless, I couldn't stop, even if I wanted to.

He presses my hips down again, guides me over him, and then he lets out a long, low growl.

The sound vibrates over me and sends a zing straight through me, all the way down to my core. I cry out again. I can't stop. I'm rocking against him, riding him, and there's so much pleasure in pressing against him, tasting him, being with him. I grip his shoulders.

"Nathaniel," I say against his mouth.

He grabs my lips for another kiss.

Then he strokes his hand lightly over my breasts, and I'm done. I can't hang on anymore. I explode in a whirlwind of sensation. I cry out, rub myself against him, try to hang on to him as I climax. The world spins out of control and he pulls me down to him.

My heart beats loudly in my ears.

That was...that was...

Slowly the world stops spinning and comes back into focus. I blink and shake my head.

My word.

*Nathaniel.*

Then the realization comes that I'm on the ground, on top of Nathaniel, in public, with his girlfriend standing thirty feet away.

Good lord. What did I just do?

My body goes from languid afterglow to icy dread in a split second. I turn my head and peer through my hair. They're not there. Thank goodness. I let out a long, relieved sigh.

"They've gone," I say.

Quickly, I roll off of Nathaniel and sit in the grass next to him.

He sits up slowly. I glance at him, then away. He looks stunned. The shell-shocked kind of stunned.

I grip the grass in my fingers, the smell of cool autumn dirt fans upward. It sends the last of my afterglow plummeting back down to earth. The chocolate and coffee flavor of Nathaniel is replaced with a bitter, grieving taste.

Nathaniel clears his throat. "Izzy?" he says hesitantly.

Oh no. Here it comes. The "Gertrude is my soul mate" bit. The "I thought you said you wouldn't maul me" bit. The "that was a mistake, let's stay friends" bit.

I stand abruptly and smack the grass and dirt off of my new jeans. Nathaniel stands up too and gives me a wary look.

What am I doing? What am I doing?

I guess, what I've always done.

I paste on a chipper smile and turn up the sass. "Well, you were right, Nathaniel. You definitely don't need any help in the sex department."

He frowns at me. A little line appears between his eyebrows and it looks like he's going to argue.

I don't want to argue. I don't want to talk about it.

I pick up a chocolate from the grass. "Do you think these are still good?"

"Izzy," he says again.

I grab another chocolate and pop it in my mouth. Mmm. "Yup. Still good."

"Izzy."

My chest aches. I turn around. "What?" I ask, feeling sharp and prickly, and unaccountably angry. I hold myself tense and wait for whatever blow he's about to deal.

"You...you're a good friend," he finally says.

My shoulders slump. That's not what I thought he was going to say. My throat aches. "Oh. Okay."

He bends down and picks up a chocolate. He holds it out to me, and I reach to take it. At the last second, he pops it in his mouth.

"Hey. That's not nice," I cry.

He winks at me and chews the chocolate with relish.

I shake my head at him and then say, "You've got grass in your hair."

He laughs at me as I stalk away from him and head up the street toward...well, toward letting go.

## 23

NATHANIEL

I CATCH UP TO IZZY AS SHE HURRIES UP MAIN STREET TOWARD the resort.

She's moving so fast it's almost like she's running from something. I snort. She could be running from the fact that we almost did the dirty in public, in front of Gertrude, Raphael, all of Romeo.

My mind spins in circles, trying to make sense of this, but I can't.

There's no logical way to explain how one second I can be in complete control of my faculties and the next I've lost my mind and all I can think of is how much I want to touch Izzy. Kiss Izzy. Make her laugh. Have fun with her. Be with her.

It doesn't make any sense.

Which means it has to be the stress of the weekend, or the environment, or mistaking friendship for something more.

The fact that we shared the most mind-blowing kiss of my life, that Izzy orgasmed and I nearly lost it too, means nothing.

Nothing at all.

Nothing's changed. I still want Gertrude, my soul mate, back. Izzy is still hung up on her ex. The only thing to do is put that kiss behind us and pretend it never happened.

Easy.

We're nearing the end of Main Street, and there's a dance studio with big glass windows. The door's open and waltz music drifts out to the sidewalk.

I glance over at Izzy. Her cheeks are pink and I can tell she's turning something over in her mind. She hasn't looked at me since I caught up.

"Hey," I say.

She turns toward me, but when she does, her eyes go wide. She grabs my arm and yanks me back from the windows of the dance studio. She pushes me against the brick wall. It's amazing, for a woman nearly a foot shorter than me, she certainly has a lot of strength when she wants to use it.

"They're in there," she says. She nods at the open studio door. I can hear a woman clapping in time to the music and counting, "One, two, three, four, five, six."

"Dancing? Gertrude doesn't dance," I say. I peer around the window molding into the studio. Quickly I pull back.

Gertrude's spinning in Raphael's arms in the middle of

the wooden dance floor.

Izzy leans to the side and looks in the studio then pulls back. "Well, she dances now."

I chew on that.

Izzy takes another quick look, then grabs my hand and tugs me away from the wall. I smile down at her hand in mine and shake my head in bemusement.

If I remember correctly, the way she's holding my hand means "we're comfortable together." My hand tingles and my body goes tense. I'm not sure *comfortable* is a word I'd use in the same sentence as *together* and *Izzy*.

She pulls me down a small alley and around the back of the studio. Then we're past the studio and heading up the hill toward the resort.

"This is good news," Izzy says. She pulls her hand out of mine.

"What's good news?"

I study her. It seems like she's put behind whatever was bothering her after our kiss. The familiar mischief-making spark is back in her eyes and there's a bounce in her step.

"The dancing." She spins in a circle.

I watch as the breeze picks up her hair and it flies around her. She laughs as it blows into her eyes and she bats it aside.

There's a grassy meadow to the right of us with goldenrod and yellow coneflowers and wild daisies. I can smell the flowers and the sweetness of green grass with its dew recently evaporated in the morning sun.

"What about the dancing?" I roll my shoulders and tilt my face up to the sky.

I should take vacations more often. I've been in the city,

in my office for so long, I'd forgotten what grass smelled like, and what the sun feels like, or even what someone's genuine laugh sounds like.

Izzy stops spinning. She wobbles a bit and sways. "I'm dizzy."

"The dancing?" I urge her.

She steadies herself and smiles up at me. "Exactly. You're going to win Gertrude back at the dance."

I stop walking and fold my arms across my chest. "What dance? The wedding dance? Isn't that a little late?"

She looks at me like I'm missing the point. "There's a dance tonight at the resort. It's called Dance Under the Stars. Didn't you see the activities flyer?"

"Why would I look at the activities flyer? I'm trying to win back my girlfriend, not go on a birding hike."

Izzy grins at me. "Oookay then."

We start walking again.

"Anyway," says Izzy. "Tonight is the night. You're ready. You look great, you've got touch, you've got compliments, you've got mystery, the dance will be the perfect romantic environment. It'll be wonderful. There's no way you won't succeed."

I look at her from the side of my eye. She looks absolutely convinced that I'm going to win back Gertrude. I shake my head.

"There's just one problem," I say.

"What?" Izzy wrinkles her brow.

I gesture at myself. "Me. I can't dance."

Izzy's eyes widen. "Ohhhh."

I nod. Exactly.

## 24

---



We find a secluded copse of pine trees down the mountain not far from the resort.

The pine trees form a perfect enclosure with a twenty foot wide circle in the middle. The pine needles make a soft carpet that prevents any undergrowth. They crackle under my feet and send up the scent of a Christmas tree heavily laden with ornaments.

"It's like a little forest room," Izzy says.

She spins around and takes in the shelter of green pines surrounding us, and the bright blue sky above us.

There are the noises of the forest, a chattering squirrel, a snapping branch, and a high bird song, but otherwise, it feels like Izzy and I are all alone in the world.

Which is good. Because dancing and I don't get along.

Izzy stops spinning and holds her hand out to me. "Shall we?"

There's an amused smile on her face. "What's so funny?" I ask.

I put my hand in hers. An electric tingle flows through me. I grip her hand more tightly as she comes closer.

"I was just thinking how much taller you are than me. We don't really fit, do we?" She glances up at me with an amused smile.

Immediately, I think of her lying on top of me in the park.

"We fit fine," I say. Then I scowl, because why am I thinking of the park?

She lifts an eyebrow and I try not to let on what image just flashed in my mind.

"What I meant is, we don't have to fit for you to teach me to dance." I look down at her and try to radiate confidence and calm. Then, I admit, "I'm a terrible dancer."

She takes my hand and positions it over her lower back. "I thought you said you didn't know how?"

"I don't. I just figured, I'm probably terrible."

I'm having trouble thinking because my hand is in the same spot it was in during our kiss in the park. There's a soft curve at the base of her spine, and she's warm and close.

She takes my other hand and holds it in her own. I draw in a long, Christmas-scented breath. Izzy stands so close that there's only a whisper between us. I have the irresistible urge to close the gap and pull her to me.

She lifts her chin and looks up at me, and I can tell she feels the magnetism too.

"You'll do great," she says. Her voice breaks a bit.

"Why do you say that?"

She starts to sway and I move with her.

"Because dancing mirrors making love, and you don't need any help in that department, remember? If you have the right partner, dancing is easy." Her lips turn into a wry, humor-filled smile.

Her long hair falls over her eyes, so I unclasp our hands and gently tuck her hair back behind her ear. My hand brushes the soft edge of her ear and the line of her jaw.

She stops swaying and gives me a stunned look. "Why'd you do that?"

I swallow, suddenly self-conscious and confused. "I…" I shrug. I don't know why I did it, it just felt right. "I'm sorry?"

For a second she looks upset, but then she shrugs it off. "Come on. Dancing."

She holds her hand up and I take it. I look over her head at the pine trees, the fallen limbs covered in moss, the ferns, and the small boulders strewn over the ground. The forest is simple. Tree, moss, rock. I thought Izzy was simple like the forest, but she's not.

I frown at a pine cone. It doesn't matter whether she's simple or complex. I won't see her after tonight.

She starts to move again. "Pay attention," she says.

I turn my gaze back down to her.

"Good," she says.

Izzy starts to hum, I don't know the tune, but it's slow and sweet. Her hand spreads over my back and I get lost in the moment.

"Dancing is one of the most intimate things you can do with someone," Izzy says.

I resist the urge to run my fingers across Izzy's back and concentrate on moving with her.

"You can dance fast with energy, like a quickie against a wall, or you can dance slow and lingering, like a night of foreplay and..."

I stare at her lips, at the little heart freckle above them. She licks her bottom lip and I hold back a groan. She notices my expression and frowns.

"We don't have time to learn steps, and positions, so I want you to dance intuitively. Tonight, when you ask Gertrude to dance, you need to lead her to the floor, take her in your arms, press your body gently to hers, and show her in your touch and in your movement how much you love her. How right for each other you are."

Izzy swallows and I watch her throat bob. My gaze catches on the little dip at the base of her throat that I lingered at last night.

"That's all?" I ask.

Izzy nods. "Easy peasy," she says.

Then, for some reason, there isn't any space between us. Our bodies are touching and my hand is spread over her back and we're swaying to the song that Izzy's no longer humming.

The soft carpet of pine needles crackles below us. It's a soft cushion that I slowly spin Izzy across. She keeps ahold of my gaze, and I lead us around the copse.

She's right. Dancing is intimate. Dancing feels like love.

I don't know why I've never danced before. I don't know why I never danced with Gertrude.

Gertrude.

I frown at Izzy. There's something sharp poking me. It feels like a pine needle, but it's on the inside. "What are you doing after all this?" I ask.

Izzy blinks and her eyes go from soft to focused. "All what?"

"Tomorrow, when Gertrude and I are together, back in New York. What will you do?" For some reason, my chest aches at the thought of tomorrow. Like I don't want it to come. Which is ridiculous.

She beams up at me. "Oh, you know me. I'll just keep skipping along. Hopping from one thing to the next."

Since we're close, and I'm holding Izzy against me, I can feel the tension in her and I know instinctively that her smile is forced. I rub my thumb comfortingly over her back.

"Do you think you'll ever settle down?" I ask.

Then I hold my breath. Which makes me realize how much I care about her answer.

She gives me an ironic smile. Then she says, "No."

I let out my breath and spin her in a circle.

We're silent for a moment, and the dance is no longer languid. There's tension where our bodies meet.

I realize that's ridiculous. What does it matter if she doesn't settle down? She's not my soul mate. She's not my love. It has nothing to do with me.

She must have come to the same conclusion, because she squeezes my hand and says, "What about you? Are you ever going to step off that life path you planned and have a little adventure?"

I huff out a small laugh and shake my head at her. "What do you think?"

Izzy tilts her chin and pretends deep thought. "No?"

She's joking, but it scares me that she might be right.

"What's wrong?" she asks when she notices my expression.

I grip her hand more tightly and spin us to the center of the pine needle circle.

"It scares me," I admit. "I didn't realize how much I'd hemmed myself in."

I look down at her to see if she's following me. She nods in understanding. I go on, "I created this life, this image of myself, and I defined myself by it. I'm in finance. I'll be a partner at my firm within five years. I date an appropriate woman. I'll propose within three years. We'll marry after a one-year engagement. Move into a place on the park. Then, in three years we'll have our first child. We'll hire a nanny that speaks multiple languages so our kid can be multi-lingual. After another two years, we'll have our second and final child. They'll get into the best private school. I'll get bigger accounts at work. Gertrude will excel at her career. We'll vacation two weeks a year in St. John, or the Hamptons. Our kids will graduate and go on to an Ivy League. Gertrude and I will retire. The next fifty years are planned out to the second. Every detail is penciled in and planned for. There'll be Thai food every Saturday and coffee every Wednesday night. It's ridiculous, isn't it?" I look at Izzy, and I know there's quiet desperation in my eyes.

She looks at me with compassion, and asks, "Is it?"

My eyes sting, maybe from scent of pine needles, maybe not. My lips twist. "I just wanted to live a good life. To succeed. To be happy."

Izzy nods and then rests her head against my chest.

"I think I should be more like you," I say.

She lets out a small laugh. "No. Don't do that. You're perfect as you are."

I look down at the top of her head in surprise but she doesn't look up.

"Mr. Serious in a suit?" I ask, remembering her description of me.

She shakes her head, "that's not you."

I think about that for a moment, and then I nod. That's not me. I stand and sway with Izzy in my arms.

"Come Monday," I finally say, "I'm going to make some changes. Like you always say, just because I started on a path doesn't mean I can't take an exit lane."

I can feel her smiling against me.

"What about you?" I ask.

Finally, she looks up at me. I hold her in the circle of my arms.

"I think I've taken too many exit lanes." Her eyes crinkle at the corners. "While you've been tying yourself down, I've been running so far, so fast that I've run out of air. Maybe neither is the best way, but c'est la vie. We do the best we can."

We stop moving and I loop my hands around her back. I tell her exactly what she told me, and I mean it, with all my heart. "Izzy, you're perfect as you are."

Her eyes twinkle. "And you, my friend, are a perfect student."

I think she means that I give great compliments. I unloop my arms and step back. The warmth I was feeling fades when I remember why we're here. For me to win Gertrude back. My soul mate. For me to carry on with my life, in the best way I know how.

# 25

Izzy

THE SUN IS DOWN AND THE BRIGHTEST STARS ARE JUST beginning to appear in the dusky blue sky.

The sounds of the jazz band playing an old favorite drift over the grassy lawn. The Dance Under the Stars has begun.

I peek around the corner of the building. There are glowing paper lanterns hung around the lawn to designate the "ballroom."

Bar-height tables with candles are set up at the edges of the dance area and a bartender behind an outdoor bar is serving wine and beer. There's even a firepit with a s'mores station for the couples that want to indulge their sweet tooth.

It's still early but there are already about two dozen couples dancing to the music. I scan the crowd and find who

I'm looking for. Raphael and Gertrude are at the outdoor bar area enjoying a bottle of wine.

I poke my head back around the corner and smirk at Nate.

He looks a little green. Like he might be sick. Maybe we shouldn't have ordered room service dinner before coming down.

"Is she there?" he asks.

I put my hand on his arm and squeeze. "Yup. Don't worry. You've got this." I ignore the clenching in my stomach that signals I wish that he didn't.

He looks down at my hand and then nods at me. "Alright." The look in his eyes makes my stomach clench even harder. "How does she look?"

I peer around the corner again and take Gertrude in. I scowl. How does she look? She looks like the woman who has Nate's heart. What else is there to say?

When I come back around, he says, "Well?"

I shrug. "She looks ready to be swept off her feet by her soul mate."

Nathaniel's shoulders relax a bit and he loses some of the tension around his mouth. "How are you going to get Raphael out of the way? You never did say."

I reach up and straighten Nate's collar. My job tonight is to pull Raphael away from Gertrude and distract him enough for Nate to slip in and win Gertrude back.

I lift an eyebrow. "Have you learned nothing about me in the past few days?" I pat his cheek. "Give me five minutes and the coast'll be clear."

His eyes crinkle in amusement. "Are you sure you even need five? I'm pretty certain you bowled me over in two."

My chest expands in happiness at the smile on his face. My fingers rest on the rough stubble of his cheek. He closes his own hand over mine.

The jazz band begins a romantic slow melody perfect for dancing. My stomach loosens and a warmth pools low in my abdomen. Nate's hand is warm over mine. Even though the autumn evening is cool, I feel warm standing so close to him. The music wraps around us and it feels as if we should be dancing.

We don't.

The time for dancing is past.

Nathaniel's eyes flicker. I see a shade of doubt enter them. "Izzy?"

My throat tightens.

"Will I see you? After?" he asks.

I blink at the sudden stinging in my eyes. My lip starts to wobble, so I smile up at him. "Did you know I hate goodbyes? I can't seem to figure out how to let go."

I shrug and my heart feels as if it's cracking open and spilling all its contents into the grass. "For some reason, I find it almost impossible to let go of dreams, even when they can't possibly come true. Especially when they can't come true."

Nate frowns and pulls his hand from mine. I shiver as the night air seeps through my sweater.

"Izzy..."

I drop my hand from his cheek and clench it by my side.

The night frogs by the lake have started singing, and they blend with the beat of the jazz band.

"So this is it then?" He stares at me with quiet intensity. It feels like he expects me to say no, that I'll be here in the morning to con chocolate croissants out of him. But really, that's not how this works.

I've helped him win Gertrude, and he's helped me.

"This is it," I agree.

His jaw tightens and I see a bit of the serious Nate in him. He holds out his hand to me, his palm open. I look down at it and then up at him and frown.

"What?"

His lips curl up at the corners. "This is me asking you to dance, Izzy. This is where you say yes."

I give him an answering smile, and suddenly, even though this moment is bittersweet, it still feels wonderful.

"Alright then," I say.

I set my hand in Nate's and he pulls me to him. He's warm, and firm, and comforting.

I press my head to his chest and listen to his heartbeat through all the layers of his clothing. His hands stroke up and down my back as we sway to the music and listen to the night sounds. I relax into him and close my eyes so that I can remember every touch, every scent, every sound.

The song is coming to its final refrain, the chords soft and slow. I don't want this moment to end, but that's how life is, isn't it? Moments end and new ones begin.

The music stops and Nate stops with it. We stand still in each other's arms.

I lift my head from his chest and say, "I put my backpack at the concierge desk while you were in the shower. So when you and Gertrude get all...hot and heavy, you can go back to your room. You don't have to worry that I'll be there."

He shifts and I know he's looking down at me, trying to see my expression. I keep my head tilted down.

"Where will you sleep?" he asks.

"Don't worry about me. Worry about yourself." I lift my chin and look at the darkening sky. More stars have appeared. One of them winks at me.

"What if this doesn't work? What if Gertrude—"

"She loves you," I say firmly. "The second she sees you, she'll realize the mistake she's made. You were right. All it will take is seeing you. You're kind, you're loyal, you're patient and forgiving, you're incredibly decent, you would give a stranger the shirt off your back." I smile. "Actually, you did give a stranger the shirt off your back. Any woman would be lucky to love you. To have your love in return. Gertrude knows this. She loves you, because when you smile, it's always genuine, and not given out willy-nilly. She loves you because you'd try to protect her even when she's being hardheaded and doing stupid things. She loves you because you are determined and focused, but also easy-going enough to go along with a bit of fun. She..." I trail off because Nate's watching me with a funny expression on his face.

"Is that what you think?" he asks.

My heart thuds. I step out of his arms into the chilly night. "Yes. I think Gertrude loves you for all those reasons."

"Right," Nate says slowly. His brows lower and he frowns.

It feels like a fist grips my heart and squeezes painfully. I take another step back.

"Look," I say, "we don't have time for this. Your Gertrude is down there with Raphael. He's wooing her with wine and words and romance. It's time for you to reclaim your destiny."

I gesture toward the Dance Under the Stars. The Chinese lanterns shine bright in the dark, like a beacon.

"Give me five minutes to get Raphael out of the way," I say. "Then do what we practiced. Touch, compliments, gifts, environment, dance. Got it?"

I give him a bright smile.

"Got it," he says solemnly. Then he steps forward, closer to me. "Izzy?" He takes another step closer. The air warms between us.

"Yes?"

He touches the edge of my jaw. "Thank you."

The second he says those words, I know. He *was* my sign, this was the right thing to do, everything is going to come out okay. Everything will be okay. The universe gave me Nate right when I needed him. And apparently, the universe gave me to Nate right when he needed me. Everything is going to work out. It'll be hard, but things always get harder before they get better.

"No. Thank you," I say.

Then I grasp his arms, stand on my tiptoes and kiss him at the edge of his mouth.

He stiffens with surprise and his mouth tightens before relaxing under mine. He brushes his hands over my arms as I let myself linger for a moment. Then I pull away.

"You'll never know how much this has meant to me," I tell him.

Let that be my goodbye.

I lift my hand and then turn away from him. I put a bounce in my step as I walk down the grassy slope toward the end of something good.

**26**

—————

Izzy

I zero in on Raphael and Gertrude snuggled up at their table. Hmm. How to separate them as quickly as possible?

I weave through the crowd, and try not to think about Nate and the fact that this is goodbye. No matter that I don't want to say it out loud, a goodbye is a goodbye.

I have the sudden urge to turn around, run back up the slope and tell Nathaniel that... My mind refuses to complete the thought.

Tell him what?

I pause and look down at the grass and the pattern of shadows that the Chinese lanterns create. Tell him...

I close my eyes.

Nothing. Tell him nothing.

I open my eyes and pick my way toward the bar. I

promised Nate that I'd help him win back Gertrude, so that's what I'm going to do.

It doesn't matter if it hurts, or feels like a breaking heart. Sometimes what feels wrong is right. Like rebreaking a bone to help it heal properly. I've been needing to rebreak this bone for a long while now.

Up ahead, Raphael runs his hand proprietarily over Gertrude's back. She leans into his side and rests her head on his shoulder.

I move closer to their table. Gertrude has on a strong perfume. It smells like lilies. I breathe through my mouth. I hate the smell of lilies, it always reminds me of funerals and the massive obligatory lily bouquets. Their smell lingers long after the burial. Yuck.

"We're getting married tomorrow," Gertrude says in a quivering voice. Is that trepidation I hear? Maybe this'll be easier than I thought.

"And all my dreams will come true, my treasure." Raphael lifts her hand and kisses it.

Oh, he's good. He really is good.

But, honestly, this isn't anything a bit of chaos can't handle.

Raphael lifts his wine glass. "A toast, to my beautiful, sexy, insatiable wife-to-be."

Gertrude raises her glass and taps it against Raphael's with a tinkling clank. I'm right behind them. It's game time.

For the benefit of anyone watching, I pretend to stumble. I turn my ankle and then cry out. My arms flail in the air and then I smack into Gertrude.

She gives a loud, shocked gasp and falls back into

Raphael. I let out another squeak for good measure and then pretend to try to steady myself. Instead I swipe at her glass. The red wine spills all over the front of her white wrap dress. It's a splattery, gross mess. But maybe it's not good enough.

"Oh, oh, no!" I cry out. I fall backward and pretend to grasp at the table. Instead I bat at the half-full bottle of wine. It flips over and a near geyser of wine splashes out and covers Gertrude from her head to her feet.

Her dress looks like a gruesome Jackson Pollock painting.

I grasp the edge of the table. I don't have to fake the stunned expression on my face. Gertrude looks like a sopping wet, wine-soaked disaster.

"I'm...I'm so sorry," I say.

And truly I am. How did she get herself into this mess? How was she possibly lured away from Nate?

Gertrude's mouth opens then closes, then opens. She looks like a fish trying to breathe on land.

"Oh how terrible. My treasure," Raphael says with a great deal of sympathy in his voice.

The sympathy is ruined though when I notice that he's carefully backing away from her. Apparently, he doesn't want to get wine on his silk shirt.

Gertrude finally comes out of her stunned state. She looks down at herself and lets out a muffled shriek. Then she shakes her arms and wine drops fly through the air.

"You..." She thrusts a finger at me.

I take a step back. "Me?"

I look around, a few of the couples have stopped dancing to stare.

"What's wrong with you? Can't you watch where you're going? Are you drunk? An idiot?" Her face is pinched and angry.

Poor Gertrude, I think she must be under a lot of stress.

"I'm really sorry," I say again. "Let me help."

I pick up some cold, wine-soaked napkins and hold them out to her. "We could dab your dress."

Wine droplets run down my hand. Gertrude looks at me like I'm holding a snake. "Get those away from me."

I drop them back to the table. They hit with a squelch.

"My treasure," Raphael says.

Gertrude swings toward him. "What?" Then, she must realize that she sounds really angry, because her lower lip wobbles and she looks like she's about to cry.

Poor Gertrude. Now I almost feel bad about ruining her dress. But, really, it's for her greater good. Nate is waiting, just around the corner, ready to sweep her off her wine-soaked feet.

Raphael holds up his hands in a consoling gesture. "Please, my treasure, why don't you go to the room and repair yourself? A new dress, no? You will be even more beautiful, I'm sure. I'll clean everything here and order a new bottle of wine. I will buy you a hundred dresses tomorrow. A wedding gift."

I watch Gertrude to see if she's taking in what he's dealing out. She is. Her face softens and she nods. "You're right. Of course. I'll be back."

She gives me a withering stare and then strides away. I watch her until she disappears through the main lobby's door. Then, I turn back to Raphael. He's busy signaling the waitstaff to come clean up the mess I made.

I look down at my watch. It's been three minutes since I left Nate. I work faster than I thought. Now, it's time to take Raphael completely out of the picture.

I reach out and gently touch my fingers to the back of Raphael's hand.

He swings back to me, an irritated look on his face. But when he sees my expression, the irritated look immediately shifts to solicitude.

I use all the sugar and honey that was bred into me as a southern girl and I pour it on him.

"Excuse me? Are you Italian? I just love Italians."

Raphael's eyes light with interest. "I am Italian."

I force myself not to look back at the resort, to where Nate and Gertrude are having their reunion. I have a job to do.

"Have you ever been to Venice?" I ask.

Raphael gives a gasp of pleasure. "Why, that is the place of my birth. My first love."

Uh huh.

I bat my eyelashes. "Oh that's just wonderful! Then you'll definitely be able to solve my problem."

I come around the table and loop my arm through Raphael's.

"It's just over here. It'll only take a few moments." I start to lead him down to the lake, but he hesitates, looking back at his table.

"Don't you worry," I reassure him, "we'll be back in a jiffy.

You won't miss your lady love. I'm ever so grateful you're helping me." I squeeze his arm.

Okay, I think I'm laying it on a little too thick. But, Raphael doesn't seem to notice. He acquiesces and we head down to the lake. When we get there, I notice a thin fog rising from the water and spreading over the grass and the boats.

"What is it I can help you with?" Raphael asks when we arrive at the lake. He looks up again toward the lanterns and the dance.

"Welllll." Okay, this is where I improvise. I look at the boats. Hmm. "I wanted to have a romantic, moonlit boat ride with my love. But he's left me." My voice breaks on the last bit, and I sound even sadder than I realized I would.

Raphael frowns at me. "You've lost your love?"

I nod and my whole body feels heavy. "I have."

"I am sorry."

I look at the lake, covered in fog, all the memories buried underneath. "Will you take me around? Just once?"

Raphael glances back toward the dance. I do too. Gertrude isn't back yet. In fact, if everything goes according to plan, she won't come back at all.

"Alright, little one," Raphael says.

I try not to scowl. Apparently, he likes to give women pet names.

Raphael flips over one of the rowboats and positions it in the water.

"After you." He gestures to the boat.

I climb in. Then, for the next twenty minutes, I somehow confuse Raphael enough to keep rowing us in circles. By the time we climb out of the boat, I'm freezing from the fog and Raphael is irritable from being kept from Gertrude. I hurry after him as he stalks up the hill.

"I can't walk so fast," I say, trying to get him to slow down. I don't want him to interrupt Nate and Gertrude at a crucial moment. "Slow down, please."

"I'm sorry, little one, I must return to my treasure." He hurries toward the dance. Even when irritated he's suave.

I jog after him. If I see Nate and Gertrude dancing I'm fully prepared to dive in front of Raphael and trip him.

Luckily, when we arrive back at the Dance Under the Stars, Nate and Gertrude are nowhere to be found. The table with the wine spill is completely clean and the dance is in full swing.

But no Gertrude. And no Nate.

"She must be in the room," Raphael says. He turns toward the resort.

"I'll go with you," I say.

He turns and frowns at me. "But why?"

Oh. "Um. To apologize," I say. "I really, really want to apologize. Again."

Raphael shrugs and walks toward the front entrance. I hurry after him. The jazz music fades and the light gets brighter as we make it to the doors. Raphael pulls them open. He's on a mission. I slip in after him and follow him to his room.

At the door, he opens it and calls out, "My treasure, where are you?"

I let out a sigh of relief because the room is empty. Raphael's treasure is gone and back where she belongs.

Raphael turns to me with a look of consternation.

I smile at him. "Perhaps she's back at the dance."

But I know she won't be.

As I wander back toward the lobby, I glance out one of the side windows. There, framed in the moonlight, is Nate. He holds Gertrude in his arms. He turns her face up to him, and then... I want to look away, I really should look away, but I can't.

He kisses her.

It's sweet. They look happy. Like two lovers kissing in the moonlight.

I wipe at my eyes and turn away.

I'm happy for him. I really am.

I watch as Raphael hurries out the front door and down toward the dance. He won't see Nate and Gertrude. They're on the other side of the building.

Everything has turned out for the best.

I lift my chin and put a smile on my face.

Then I pick up my backpack from behind the front desk. It's not a far walk to downtown Romeo. I can sleep at the bus stop. It has a wooden bench that's calling my name.

**27**

———

Nathaniel

Wow.

When Izzy said "give me five minutes to get Raphael out of the way" she actually meant "give me two minutes to cause massive chaos."

I grin as I think of her perfectly choreographed wine spill. I don't know how she does it. Then, my grin fades as I remember that I won't get to see her make trouble ever again. She's gone off somewhere with Raphael and I'm waiting for Gertrude to come back outside.

Unfortunately, the excitement I should be feeling about finally speaking with Gertrude is eclipsed by the ache in my chest from the idea of never seeing Izzy again.

I run my hand through my hair and try not to worry. This is right. When Gertrude sees me she'll remember why we're good together, and when I see Gertrude, I'll remember the same.

I need the reminder, because right now all I want to do is run down the slope and tear Izzy away from Raphael. But this moment is about Gertrude, not Izzy. All this has been for Gertrude.

Hasn't it?

I lean back against a wooden column near the side entrance of the resort and let the cool breeze calm my mind. It's fine. Erma even said that Gertrude is my soul mate. It'll all work out.

I narrow my eyes. Gertrude walks down the hallway in the tight red dress that she was wearing in the café. Once again her auburn hair is piled on top of her head. The neckline of her dress forms a heart shape that dips low to her cleavage. She looks beautiful.

She opens the door and steps onto the flagstone path leading down the lawn toward the dance. She doesn't notice me. She's focused on the lights of the dance below.

I push away from the column. When I do, Gertrude notices my movement. She looks toward me then gasps.

"Nathaniel?"

I smile at her. "Hi, Gertrude."

She stands completely still and stares at me with a shocked expression.

I take the final few steps toward her.

My shoes echo on the flagstone. The jazz band plays a song about love, the stars are out, and the breeze is light. It's the perfect environment for romance.

"You look beautiful," I say.

And I mean it, Gertrude always looks lovely. Except, now I notice that she also always looks, how did Izzy put it? Kinda wound tight. My smile widens at the thought.

When it does, Gertrude's eyebrows climb in surprise. "What happened to you?" she blurts out.

She gestures at my casual clothing and my expression. It's not surprising. In our three years together I don't think Gertrude ever saw me in anything but a suit. And I'm not sure she ever really saw me smile.

I look down at myself. I don't feel any different, in fact, I feel more like me than I have in years.

What happened to me?

Izzy happened to me.

But I don't think I can say that. So, instead I say, "I took a vacation."

"A vacation? When have you ever taken a vacation? Nathaniel, are you feeling okay?" Gertrude steps forward and puts her hand to my forehead.

When she does, I expect to feel something, some spark from her touch. But the only thing I feel is the cold dampness of her fingers.

I take her hand and pull it away from my head. "I feel fine. Actually, I feel better than I have in years."

I hold her hand in mine. Her fingers are clammy. She frowns at me again.

The jazz band starts another song. This is the moment where I should ask her to dance. Instead, I pull her up the flagstone path, away from the lanterns and the music. There's a little circular herb garden with a stone sundial and a large rectangular window looking into the lobby. The garden is bathed in silver moonlight.

"Nathaniel, if this is about Raphael..." Gertrude hesitates, so I put my hand on her arm comfortingly. It seems I've picked up a few habits from Izzy.

"I was going to propose to you this weekend," I say.

Gertrude's face flushes red enough for me to see in the low light. "You were?"

I nod, "but I'm glad I didn't."

"You are?" She shifts on her high heels and frowns at me.

I nod again. "I realize I've been living this fixed path. But who fixed it? Me." I gesture to myself. "I really have to thank you." I squeeze her hand.

"You do?" she asks. She seems slightly confused, which isn't normal for Gertrude.

"I do. If you hadn't left with Raphael, I never would've realized how I penned myself in. Now I see how much there is before me. How much more the world has to offer." I think about everything I've experienced. "There are walks in the country, long bus rides, old farmhouses with squeaky beds, chocolate croissants and coffee, dancing in the forest, moonlit boat rides with poetry, there's laughter and adventures and if you hadn't left, I would never have come to Romeo, I would never have met..." I trail off.

"Met?" asks Gertrude with a frown.

My chest constricts. "Do you believe in fate?" I search her expression. Gertrude is supposedly my soul mate, my fated true love. But...

Gertrude lets out a short, barking laugh. "Nathaniel. What happened to you? You're so different."

I shake my head.

She holds up her hand and pulls me toward her. "No. I like it. Why weren't you like this before? Boat rides in the moonlight. What's gotten into you?"

She places her hands on my chest and looks up at me. The moonlight glows on her pale skin and turns her green eyes luminescent. She gives me the look I was hoping for. The one that tells me that she still wants me and that Raphael was a mistake.

"You've changed," she says.

"Have I?"

"I like it," she says, "I was just thinking that maybe I made a mistake. Done something rash and stupid. That maybe you were right. And then here you are, better than ever."

I think of Izzy's words, that I've always been like this, that I'm perfect as I am.

Gertrude rubs her hands slowly up and down my chest. Then she wraps her hands around my back. In the language of touch she'd be saying, "I want you back." I put my hands on her arms and hold her too.

"Nathaniel, will you kiss me?" she asks.

I look down at Gertrude and I think back on the last three years. I don't remember smiling, or laughing, or even living. What exactly did we have together? What was I holding on to so hard?

"Nathaniel?" she waits expectantly, her face turned up.

"Of course," I say. I swallow back the feeling of wrongness and drift my hand over her jaw and tilt her chin up. Then I kiss her.

Gertrude's lips are clammy and dry. She leans against me and I grip her arms. I tilt my chin and continue the kiss, but the longer it goes on the worse I feel. This is wrong. It's all wrong. This kiss has left me completely cold.

Slowly, and carefully, I step back from Gertrude.

She pats her cheeks and then straightens her dress. "Let's go to your room," she says. "Well talk this through." She trails her eyes down my chest. "We'll do more."

There's a bad taste in my mouth at the thought. "Gertrude?"

"Yes?"

"Why exactly do you love me?"

"What?" she asks. Her mouth forms a little O of surprise.

"It's a fairly simple question," I say. "I don't need a big list."

Her nostrils flare and she taps her heel impatiently on the flagstone. "Well, I..." She narrows her eyes. "I like your career trajectory."

I can't take fault with her, because her words are almost identical to what I said about her only a few days ago. However... "I'm going to quit my job."

"What?" she says in surprise.

I nod. "What else?"

She looks around, as if she's searching for a clue. "I like your plans for the future. A penthouse on the park and vacations in St. John's."

My chest loosens as a feeling of relief starts to flow through me. "I don't think I want that anymore," I admit.

Gertrude crosses her arms over her chest and taps her heel more loudly. "You don't?" she asks sharply.

I shake my head no as a wide smile spreads across my face.

She looks exasperatedly around the little moonlit garden. "Well, I love that you have an MBA from—"

"Gertrude," I say.

She stops talking and frowns at me. Her lower lip pushes out and her forehead wrinkles. "What?"

"Do you love when I smile? Because it's genuine and not given willy-nilly?" I ask.

"Why would I love when you smile? Why would I care if you're smiling or not? What does that have to do with anything?"

I nod happily. "Exactly. But do you love that I'd give a stranger the shirt off my back?"

She narrows her eyes. "Did you get a charitable contribution receipt for taxes?"

I can't help it, I laugh. And once I start I can't stop. It's ridiculous. It's all so ridiculous.

"Nathaniel, what? What's so funny?"

I take Gertrude in my arms and spin her around.

"Put me down." She smacks at my chest.

I set her down and grin at her. I'm dizzy and I feel like I'm floating. The only other time I feel dizzy is when I'm with Izzy. So feeling this way feels right.

"You've lost your mind," Gertrude says. She scowls at me and pats her hair back into place.

"Uh huh," I say, mimicking Izzy. Losing my mind feels amazing. "I have one last question."

"What?" Gertrude asks. She stabs bobby pins into her hair, pinning her bun back into place.

"Why did you run off with Raphael?"

Gertrude slowly lowers her hands. Her face softens imperceptibly and her eyes go slightly out of focus.

Ah. I see.

If a nightingale started singing and night moths started twittering around her head I wouldn't be surprised.

Gertrude really is in love.

"I think you should go find Raphael," I say.

Gertrude shakes herself and looks at me sharply. "Why?"

"Because he makes you happy," I say.

Gertrude frowns. "But you could too."

"No, I couldn't," I say, and we both know that's true.

"I really am sorry," Gertrude whispers, and there's genuine regret in her eyes. "I really was having second thoughts." She clears her throat and then says again, "I'm sorry."

"Don't be. Just because we chose a path doesn't mean we can't choose another."

Her eyebrows lower at this, but then she nods. "Thank you, Nathaniel," she says.

"It's Nate," I say.

But she doesn't hear me. She's already hurrying down the path toward the Dance Under the Stars and Raphael.

"Good luck," I call after her.

Then I hurry inside to find Izzy.

But, she isn't anywhere. She isn't at the dance, she isn't at the café, she isn't in the room. Finally, I stop at the front desk. Virginia is there.

"Yes, Mr. Barry?" she asks. "How may I help you?"

I clear my throat. "You haven't happened to see the

woman I've been staying with? Izzy Harris? She left her bag here, behind the desk."

Virginia nods. "Oh yes. She picked it up about ten minutes ago."

I lean forward and grasp the wood of the desk. "And did she check into another room?"

Virginia frowns down at my hands and tsks. I unlatch them and step back.

"I'm sorry, Mr. Barry, I'm not at liberty to say."

I look around the lobby, expecting to see Izzy standing behind me, with a laughing, mischievous expression. She's not there. Obviously. We said goodbye, didn't we?

A panicky feeling clutches at my throat.

Virginia watches me with a frown.

I hold out my hands to her and let the desperation I'm feeling show in my face. "Please. Can you at least tell me if she's left the resort."

Virginia thinks for a moment, she weighs me, probably trying to determine whether or not I'm a decent human being.

Finally Virginia gives a short nod. "She didn't check into another room. She's no longer a guest here."

My throat tightens even further. "Did she say where she was going?"

Virginia gives me a look that says I'm pushing it. "No."

"Okay. Thank you," I say. Then I turn and hurry out the front door. If I know Izzy, and I do, she's probably trying to hitch a ride somewhere. But if she gets in a car and rides away, I don't know if I'll ever be able to find her again.

I sprint down the road toward Romeo.

**28**

———

Nathaniel

Izzy is at the bus stop.

I slow to a walk and pull in a few deep breaths. My heart pounds from my run to town, but it feels like it's saying "thank goodness you found her." When I didn't see Izzy on the road I was terrified she was already gone.

I walk slowly toward the bus stop. Izzy lies on the wooden bench, her feet planted on the slats, with her knees up. She's using her backpack as a pillow.

I smile as a wave of relief washes over me. I found her.

The wrought-iron lampposts that line the street cast a sleepy yellow glow over us. Downtown Romeo is quiet, the shops and restaurants are closed, and the loudest noise is the bubbling of the river at the other end of Main Street. My footsteps sound overly loud as I step under the bus stop canopy.

At the noise Izzy turns her head toward me.

I grin at her. I'm so glad to see her I can't stop myself. I know it's barely been two hours since I last saw her, but it felt like a lifetime.

Her eyes widen and she scrambles to sit upright. "Nathaniel?"

My smile widens when she says my name, Nuh-thaaaan-yul. "I told you to call me Nate," I say.

She jumps up from the bench and looks around, searching for something. When she looks back at me her brows are drawn in concern.

"What happened? Where's Gertrude? Oh no, don't tell me Raphael came back. Is that it? Was there a fight? Did you punch him? Did he punch you?"

I try to hold back a laugh, but it comes out as a small, smothered noise. She's ridiculous, she's perfect. The stories she comes up with are priceless.

She takes in my expression and apparently what she sees makes her believe that everything went wrong.

"Oh no. My word, Nathaniel, last I saw you were kissing Gertrude and everything was wrapped up like a Christmas present. How could this happen? Well, don't worry, there's still time, the wedding isn't until Sunday and that means we still have at least twelve hours, maybe..."

She trails off and bites her lip. As she was talking, I kept feeling lighter and happier and more sure that this is the path for me. I don't know where it will lead, but I definitely want to take it.

I hold out my hand to her. "Izzy."

She looks down at my hand and then back up to me. Confusion flits across her face. "What are you doing?"

I look down at my open hand and then back at her. "I'm asking you to dance."

Her eyes widen and she looks around, then back at me, her expression confused.

"This is where you say yes." I smile at her.

"But, Nate." Her brows draw down and she puts her hands on her hips. "Shouldn't you be with Gertrude?"

I shake my head no.

She bites her bottom lip. "No?"

"No," I agree happily.

"But…I thought you didn't want to let her go?"

"Funny thing, letting go was a lot easier than I thought it'd be. Especially once I realized the future I'd planned wasn't the one I wanted."

"Oh," she says. Then she frowns, and instead of looking hopeful or expectant like I thought, she looks a little lost.

My elation dims a bit, and I remember that I wasn't the only one that didn't want to let go. "Izzy?"

She looks up at me, and instead of the swirl of motion and enthusiasm that I'm used to, I see a woman who is uncertain and lost.

"Yes?"

"Did you notice how beautiful Romeo is tonight?" I ask. My heart feels lodged in my throat.

She shakes her head no. "Not really."

"Have a look," I say. Slowly, I spin in a circle and she follows. "See how romantic it is? The lampposts are glowing with a soft yellow light, and look at the candles in the shop windows." I point to the electric candles in the windows of the bookshop and the bakery. Izzy moves closer to me as we keep turning. "And listen," I say, "you can still hear the crickets, and if you listen carefully, there's the sound of the river running over the stones." When I point toward the river, Izzy steps closer and leans into me, I wrap my arm around her and pull her to my side. She fits. Holding her close feels so right.

"What else?" she asks.

I stop turning and look up at the dark sky. "It's clear tonight. The sky's so black that it looks almost purple. There's the moon and the stars. And if you look close, you can see that it's a kissing moon."

"What's a kissing moon?" She turns her face up and there's a little smile waiting to appear at the edge of her lips.

I lift my eyebrows. "Don't you know? It's the kind of moon that everyone should kiss under at least once in their lives."

"Ah," she says.

I nod and her eyes crinkle.

"It's a perfect environment," she says.

I agree.

I pull her around and turn her to face me. Then I lift my hand and trail it down her jaw, over her cheek, and then to her lips.

She sways toward me and hesitantly raises her hand. When she rests her fingers on my chest, my heart hammers against her hand, as if it's dying to reach her. I run my fingers through her hair and push it back from her face so that I can see her better.

"Do you remember when I told you that you were the worst thing that could've happened to me?" I ask.

She looks at me with humor. "Something like that."

"Well, I want to amend that statement."

"Really?"

I nod. "Izzy, you are the best worst thing that's ever happened to me and that ever will."

She drops her head against my chest and gives the happiest, most full-bodied laugh I've ever heard her give. I gather her in my arms and savor the sound. When she finally stops she says, "Now that was a humdinger of a compliment."

Humdinger, huh? "Will you dance with me now?"

She tilts her head up and suddenly I'm dizzy again just from looking at her. Before I wasn't able to pull her close and hold her until the spinning stopped. Now I can.

"Izzy," I tell her again, "this is where you say yes."

Her eyes flicker in the moonlight, and I can't read her expression. "What are you doing, Nate?" she asks, and I know she isn't asking about the dancing or the compliments.

"Isn't it obvious?" I ask. I take her left hand and I thread my fingers through hers. "I'm telling you I love you."

Her eyes widen, and she pulls in a breath. She looks at our entwined fingers and then back up at me. I try not to hold my breath as I wait for her response. She considers me, and then she shakes her head and tsks.

"Nathaniel, I distinctly recall you saying that no one can fall in love in twelve hours. Didn't you say that?"

My breathing steadies at the humor I see in her eyes. "I did," I agree. "However, I never said you couldn't fall in love in forty-eight hours."

She holds back a laugh. I look down at my wrist where my watch used to be before it was stolen. "By my watch," I say, "it's been fifty-eight hours since we met. Which is forty-six hours and fifty-nine minutes longer than falling in love takes."

"Is that so?" she asks.

I nod confidently. "Trust me."

"I do," she says.

Then she puts her hands on my shoulders and stands on her tiptoes. Which I think in the language of Izzy means *hurry up and kiss me already.*

So I do.

**29**

———

Nathaniel

"So you finally realized you've always wanted to have sex in the woods," Izzy says.

She grins up at me from the soft loamy ground. The moonlight filters through the pine trees and paints her in soft night colors.

After long minutes of kissing at the bus stop I realized that we have a warm room with a bed and a fireplace back at the resort. However, there's a couple miles between town and the resort and those miles have proven too far.

Once we reached the point in the road near the pine grove where we had our dance lessons, I pulled Izzy into the woods and kissed her until she sank to the ground. I dropped to my knees and began to touch her in as many ways that said I love you as possible.

"I thought you might prefer a boat," she says.

She smiles up at me, but instead of mischief lighting her eyes there's a growing fiery need sparking in them.

I shake my head and trail my hands down her neck, to her shoulders and then down her arms until I land at her hands. I clasp her fingers with mine and then slowly climb over her.

"We're not having sex," I tell her.

She looks at me in surprise. "We're not?"

"We're making love," I say.

"Ah," she says.

I nod. I search her expression and there beneath the need in her eyes and the flush in her cheeks I see concern.

"What is it?" I ask.

She shakes her head.

"Tell me," I say.

She squeezes my hands and then she says, "I'm worried that I'm not...that I'm going to..."

"What?" I pull my hand from hers and brush her hair back.

"You love me," she says, a question, but not.

I look at her, surrounded by pine needles, with bits of leaves in her hair, and a flush to her cheeks. She came into my life like a whirlwind. Everything was tossed around and shaken up, but when the dust cleared, I found that what remained was all that mattered. I touch my fingers to the pink in her cheeks.

"I love you," I say.

She relaxes back into the ground and reaches up to me. When she does, she whispers, "I love you too."

That's all it takes.

I yank her sweater over her head and drop it to the ground behind her. I pull off my shirt and lay it beneath her too, piling up a bed for her. Izzy pulls her camisole off and her breasts spill out before me. I'm unbuttoning my pants, but I stop when I see her breasts lit up by the moonlight.

"My word," I say. "You're beautiful."

She flushes and then looks at my naked chest. "You're not so bad yourself." She fans herself. "Hubba hubba."

I give her an affronted look and she lets out a short laugh.

I snort, and dive at her, pushing her to the ground. "Sassy," I say. I push her hands to the ground and lower my hips to hers. "Will you be able to laugh when I'm doing this?"

She lifts her hips to mine and says, "Definitely, yes."

I flick open the button on her pants and push them down her legs. They stop at her sneakers. "Foiled," I say.

She laughs and kicks her shoes off. They fly toward the pine trees and land six feet away. Something chatters at us, and I think we've startled a nesting animal awake. It squawks and makes a racket running from the clearing.

"What kind of animal was that?" I ask.

Izzy looks at me and says with all seriousness, "A peeping Tom."

I give a full belly laugh as she kicks off her pants. My laugh chokes off as she slips out of her thong. My breath feels tight, and I'm dizzy again. Goodness, what she does to me.

"Your turn," she says.

Then she pushes me down to the ground to rest on top of her sweater and my shirt. I press my heels into the ground and clench my hands as she slowly unbuttons my pants. It takes all my willpower to stay patient, but I still kick off my shoes before she tugs my pants down fully.

She laughs, although this time, nothing rustles in the foliage.

"I think our audience is gone."

"Shame," she says.

Then she looks down at me with the most comical expression on her face, and I can't help it, I laugh. So much joy fills me that the only thing I *can* do is laugh. And finally, I understand what Izzy meant about making love and laughing. I didn't think they fit together, but they do. They fit perfectly. Sort of like Izzy and me.

"I'm going to make love to you now," I tell her.

"Ooookay," she says.

I smile. "But first, I'm going to give you the French tickle."

She snorts. "That's not a thing. I made that up!"

"Uh huh." I start to kiss down her belly. I lick at her skin and then blow on it. When I reach the parting of her thighs, I pull her legs apart and set my mouth over her, then I lift my head and blow on her.

"That tickles," she squeaks.

"That's the idea," I say. Then I press my hands into her thighs and hold her in place as she squirms against me. Soon, she's no longer squirming. She's lifting her thighs up and gripping my hair holding me in place, and making the sweetest little noises. She tastes like honey and I've never been so happy in my life.

"Nathaniel," she cries.

I suck on her harder.

"Nathaniel," she gasps. She tugs on my hair. I look up at her and grin.

"Yes?"

"Please," she whispers. And I notice that it doesn't feel like we're spinning anymore, it just feels like we're in each other's arms.

I breathe in the smell of the pine needles crushed beneath us and relish the stillness of this moment. I move up and position myself above her.

She wraps her arms around my back.

I push myself against her entrance. She's warm, and tight, and she feels like the only thing I've ever wanted. I take her hands in mine, I taste her lips, I try to touch her in as many places as possible, and only when I feel like I can't tell her in any other ways how much I love her, only then do I plunge inside.

She cries out and I kiss her when she does. She clenches around me, and sparks light in my vision. *My word.* My blood heats and my body vibrates with need. I can't go slow, I can't...I bury myself deeper. My mind goes blank. The only thing left is need. I need Izzy. I want Izzy. I love Izzy.

I love her.

I move inside her. And each movement I make, the in and out, the rocking, the kissing, the touching, each move tells her how I feel.

Pressure mounts in me, until I can't hold on anymore. I reach down and run my hands over Izzy's clit, I circle over her, until she contracts around me, clamps down on me. And when she does, she cries out, lifts her hips, and I lose control.

I lose myself in her.

"I love you," I say. "I love you."

Sparks fly across my vision, my heart pounds, and I release all my love. I give it all to her.

For a moment, we stay connected. I look into her eyes and she looks into mine. Everything is there, and I know with certainty that we're meant to be. That this is the road I want to take. Then she shifts beneath me, and I roll off of her to the coolness of the loamy forest floor. I pull Izzy to my side and we look up at the stars and the moon.

I feel like this would be the perfect moment for poetry, but I'm terrible at poetry, so instead I pull her closer and kiss her head and say, "I love you."

After all, "I love you" sounds a lot like poetry.

Izzy shifts onto her elbow and looks at me. I smile at her, and wonder if she's going to ask about heading back to the resort, but instead she says, "My bus leaves at six."

**30**

———————

Nathaniel

I couldn't convince Izzy to stay.

In fact, the more I tried to convince her, the more stubborn she got.

I tried making love in front of the fire, a massage in the jacuzzi, more making love in bed. A tray of chocolate croissants, and a list of all the reasons that she should stay a few more days in Romeo, and then, come back with me to New York.

Nothing convinced her.

Not even the fact that I loved her, and she said she loved me.

So here we are again, back from the cozy room at the resort in the pine tree copse. It's only five, so the sun has nearly two hours before it comes up. The sky is still dark although the birds are starting to sing. The magic of last night has leached out of the air.

I try one last time. "Izzy, stay. At least a few more days."

She shakes her head and drops her backpack to the ground then unzips it. "Nathaniel, it's not gonna work."

I raise my eyebrows. "It'll work, I've got it all planned out. I thought all night about how we could make this work, you'll come back to the city with me, move in to my place and find a job…"

Looking at Izzy's expression I realize what I'm doing. I'm planning again. Just like I did with Gertrude. "You don't want that?"

She shakes her head. "I can't."

I look around the glade desperately. My heart feels like it's dropping, bottoming out. When I lost Gertrude, it didn't feel anything this. Which should've made me realize far sooner we weren't meant to be. The thought of losing Izzy makes me desperate. We're on our way to the bus stop and I have nothing else to convince her to stay. I can't convince her.

She pulls a notebook, two pens, and an empty peanut butter jar out of her backpack.

"What's that?" I ask.

She smiles at me and hands me a pen. Then she tears a piece of paper from the notebook and gives me that too.

"You say you love me," she says.

"I do."

"But you and Gertrude just broke up."

I frown and shake my head. "That doesn't mean anything."

"It does. You need time to let her go. Plus, you have plans and changes you want to make in your life. A new career, maybe a new home, a new life goal. It's a whirlwind," she says, and I can't exactly argue with her, because her description of my life fits what I've been thinking.

"Alright," I say slowly.

"But perhaps it's temporary. And in a week, or a month, you'll realize this was crazy. It was just a crazy weekend, with a crazy girl, and that crazy love you felt was really nothing at all."

"I won't feel that way," I say.

She considers me and then nods. "But maybe you will. Maybe you'll realize that you liked your life the way it was, and you don't want it to change. That you don't want to go down this path after all."

I want to argue, but she holds up her hand, so I don't.

"It's okay if you feel that way." She holds up the notebook. "I thought of something," she says.

A bit of hope lights in me. "Yes?"

The sky lightens to a dusky blue, which I take as a sign.

"We'll write each other a letter. You write me a letter with everything you want to say, everything you hope for and want. And I'll write you a letter and tell you everything I want to say and everything I hope for and want." She swallows and looks at me nervously.

"And then?" I ask.

She bites her bottom lip. "And then we part ways. Go on with our lives. You do what you need to do, and I'll do what I need to do. And then in six months exactly, we'll meet back here at sunrise and we'll read the letters."

"Six months?" I ask. Six months seems like eternity. But it's not. She could be saying goodbye for forever, but she's not. My chest feels less tight and a niggle of hope comes in.

She nods. "Six months exactly. It'll be spring," she says the word "spring" with a bit of hope.

"Do you believe in fate?" I ask. I grip the pen tightly in my hand.

Izzy studies me for a moment and her expression softens. "I do. Very much so."

All the tension in me relaxes. Everything is going to work out.

"Me too," I tell her.

At that, she gives me the most beautiful smile I've ever seen. Then she stands on her tip toes and kisses me.

We sit down to write our letters. Izzy takes longer than I do. She chews on her pen, and wrinkles her forehead, and takes a long time to write down what she wants to. Me, on the other hand, I finish in thirty seconds. I only write two sentences.

*I love you.*

*Marry me.*

When she's done we fold up the letters and put them in the peanut butter jar. I dig a hole a foot deep by the largest pine tree, we drop the peanut butter jar in and then push the soil back over it. Then we put a pile of rocks over the hole so no wild animal can dig it up.

After that, we walk down the hill to Romeo.

Neither of us says much. We just hold hands.

When we get to the bus stop I ask Izzy if she needs me to buy her a ticket. She says no, that it's all been taken care of.

When the bus pulls up, I resist the urge to tell her not to go, to stay.

"Do you want my number?" I ask. I realize I don't have hers.

She shakes her head. "It's better if we don't." She looks at the bus, then back to me. The driver honks. "See you soon."

I notice that she isn't saying goodbye.

I smile and say, "'Til we meet again, Izzy."

She grins. "'Til we meet again."

She goes to kiss me, so I pick her up, wrap her legs around me and give her a kiss that both of us can remember for the next one hundred and eighty days.

The driver honks again, so I set her down. She grabs her backpack and runs light-footed to the bus. When she turns to wave there's a smile on her face. It's as bright as usual, but this time, I notice her eyes aren't smiling.

I lift my hand.

She waves and then disappears onto the bus.

I stand in the chill autumn morning air and watch the bus taillights disappear over the hill. I stand in downtown Romeo, long after the bus has gone, waiting for the sun to rise.

# 31

Izzy

It's evening by the time I make it back to Queens.

The sky is dark, there are no stars, and the tall buildings outside the subway stop create a wind tunnel that bites with its chill.

The air smells like the city, dirt, exhaust, and subway steam. There isn't a hint of pine needles or sweet grass.

When I boarded the train in Albany I expected to see Nate, but of course he wasn't there.

Instead, I shared my row with a steely-faced businesswoman with pointy elbows. She didn't order any food from the snack cart. Instead she pulled a bran muffin and an algae drink out of her briefcase. I didn't have any money to order anything, but my stomach was so knotted that I wasn't hungry anyway.

I keep my head down while I walk the darkened streets of my aunt's neighborhood. I know the way by heart. It's home, after all.

My backpack feels heavy and the closer I get, the slower I walk. Maybe I shouldn't have left Nathaniel. Maybe it wasn't the right thing to do. I stick my hand into my pocket and feel the cold hard case of my cell phone.

My chest pinches and there's that strangled, hollow feeling I've been trying to keep at bay. I walk up to my aunt's building and pull my keys out. It's a tall, yellow brick building with a dozen floors. The warm air envelops me and the smell of linoleum and paprika greets me. Her building has smelled the same for decades. The familiarness of it comforts me. I take the stairs to her floor, then let myself into her apartment.

"Aunt Gerry?" I call as I open the door.

She doesn't answer. The dogs aren't here either, they would've come running if they were.

I look around. Nothing has changed. Her apartment is still painted bright yellow, with overstuffed antique furniture, and an ornate coffee table covered in knitting magazines and half a dozen partially finished knitting projects.

"Aunt Gerry, are you home?" I quietly shut the front door behind me and lock it. There's no answer. I set my backpack by the front door and walk down the hall to my childhood bedroom.

It's dark, but the streetlights glow through the window and give enough light for me to make out the white wicker furniture and the stuffed animals of my childhood. Aunt Gerry still hasn't changed a thing.

I don't turn on the light. Instead, I sink down to the floor and lean back against the wall next to the door. I close my eyes for a minute, but when I do Nate's face pops into my mind and that panicky feeling starts up again. I open my eyes and pull my phone out of my pocket.

The screen glows and illuminates my room with an eerie blue.

I hold my finger over the voicemail. There's the message from David. My chest is tight and there's a burning ache in my throat and behind my eyes. I push play. The message begins.

"Izzy, where are you? Are you at your aunt's place?" I close my eyes at the familiar sound of David's voice. I drop my head to my knees. "I've been thinking about what you said. About how we shouldn't keep waiting to live. How if we keep delaying our dreams we'll never get them."

"I know," I whisper. "I know."

My eyes burn and my throat aches.

"I agree with you. I'm sorry we fought. You were right. Izzy, you were right. Let's forget about the year-long engagement. Let's do something crazy. Let's get married this weekend. Let's get married Sunday. We could do it in Romeo."

I hold my breath, because the ache in my throat has gotten so big that I don't know what else to do. I close my eyes and press my head against my knees.

David pauses, then he says in a quiet, reassuring voice, "I

love you, Izzy. You're going to marry me Sunday. You know that, right?"

Finally, I can't hold my breath anymore. I let it out, and when I do, it hurts. It hurts so much. I drag in another breath and it burns. The voicemail ends. I drag the replay back a few seconds and David's voice comes on again.

"I love you Izzy," David says.

I let out a sob and pull the replay back again.

"I love you, Izzy," he says.

I'm shaking so hard that I barely manage to pull the replay again.

"I love you Izzy. You're going to marry me Sunday. You know that, right?"

I pull the replay one last time. "I love you Izzy," he says.

I stop the voicemail. "I love you too," I whisper.

A few hours later when my aunt comes home she finds me sitting on the floor in the dark of my bedroom. The dogs sniff my shoes and jump against my legs. My aunt crouches down next to me. She looks at my face and then puts her hand to my shoulder, "Oh Izzy, what've you done to yourself?"

I reach for her arms, clasp her to me and she holds me tight, just like she used to. "Oh, Aunt Gerry, I've made a terrible mess of things."

The weight of it all nearly crushes me.

My aunt pats my hair and shushes me, "It's alright, Izzy. It's alright."

But it's not.

# 32

---

Nathaniel

Exactly Six Months Later...

It's six in the morning and sunrise is in fifteen minutes.

I pace around the small pine glade for the nine hundred and fifty-sixth time. I've been here for three hours.

Not that I thought Izzy would be here at three in the morning, but I had this image of her sitting at the base of the pine tree grinning up at me, saying "What took you so long?"

So, I came early.

I check my watch, the one I bought as soon as I made it back to the city last fall. Fourteen minutes until sunrise. The woods look different in the spring. Even in the gray morning light I can see little sprouts of lime green poking up from the ground, bright green buds unfurling from the trees beyond the pines and wildflowers closed up tight until the morning light has a chance to filter through the trees.

I turn around and pace to the other side of the clearing, kicking up the scent of pine needles to mix with the new growth from the rest of the forest.

Twelve minutes.

I turn to look at the pile of rocks at the base of the pine. It hasn't been disturbed, each of the rocks are stacked exactly as we left them. It's almost as if we put them there yesterday, the only way to tell the difference is the changed season. And of course, the changed me.

As soon as I got back to the city I took a long hard look at my life and my "life plan."

When I was called before the partners at Wisebrook and Bleakerman to accept the promotion to their ranks, I politely declined. Looking at the seven men stationed around the polished chrome conference table, I saw exactly what I would become if I stayed on my path. Their weekly income was more than most people made annually. However, of the seven men, each of them was either on their third or fourth wife. Two of them had already had a heart attack and all of them looked years beyond their age. If they had children, they barely saw them. They didn't take vacations, they didn't have hobbies. Their hobby was making money. So, if I became partner I could expect a minimum of three divorces, poor health, kids I never saw, no hobbies outside of work, and to never have another vacation.

I respectfully submitted my resignation.

Just like with Gertrude, it was easy to let go of years of

hard work and planning when I realized that I wasn't heading in the right direction.

At the end of the month I moved out of my apartment, bought a car and took a drive around the country. That drive lasted a few months. I visited all the places I said I'd go to someday but never made the time for.

Then I came back, relaxed and centered, with longer hair, jeans and t-shirts, and a direction for life. I started working again as a consultant. This time, I worked from my newly rented apartment, choosing my hours and keeping my client list small. I left time to take in the city and appreciate life. Sometimes, when I was walking down a crowded sidewalk, I'd think that I saw Izzy. But then I'd remember what she said about being in love.

That when you're crazy in love with someone you see them everywhere and in everything.

That's true. I did.

I saw her in everything I did, and everywhere I went I imagined how she'd react to it, and what she'd say. I wanted her with me.

I look down at my watch. Two minutes until sunrise.

I turn to the east. The sky is light grayish blue, the color of a robin's wing. There on the horizon, through the woods and down the slope, I can make out the first golden rays of the rising sun.

I turn toward the path Izzy would take to get to the copse. My chest feels tight and I have to remind myself to breathe. She'll be here any second now. Or maybe any minute. I smile to myself. Izzy isn't exactly the punctual type.

An early rising bird sings a long greeting to the morning

and another answers. I stick my hands in my pockets and watch the sun climb above the horizon. It's a beautiful spring day. The grayish blue sky turns bright.

I shift in impatience and the pine needles crackle beneath my feet. I tense when I see movement in the distance. I watch the spot carefully, but then I realize it was just the breeze blowing the branches of a tree.

I look down at my watch. Five minutes after sunrise.

That's okay.

I keep watching the woods. Waiting.

Izzy was worried that I wouldn't feel the same about her after six months. She thought that maybe I'd realize that it was just a crazy weekend with a crazy girl and the crazy love I was feeling wasn't real. That eventually I'd snap out of it and be glad to go back to my life.

She didn't need to worry.

The only thing I needed to snap out of was my old way of living and thinking.

I start to pace again. I look at my watch more often than I'd like.

Thirty minutes after sunrise.

An hour.

I sit down next to the pile of rocks and stare at the sky. The sun keeps rising higher. The day keeps getting warmer. I take off my coat and pace the clearing again.

Two hours.

I lie down on the pine needles and stare at the sky. There are wisps of clouds high up that barely move, and fluffy woolly clouds lower down that sprint past pushed by a stiff breeze.

I wonder if I got the day wrong. Maybe I'm a day early, or a day late. I look at the date on my watch. No, this is right. It's been six months exactly. I knew that though.

Four hours past sunrise.

A curious doe and her fawn walk by. I stay still, but when she sees me, her nostrils sniff the air and then she takes off, her fawn galloping after her.

Six hours.

The sun is high in the sky. There's a gnawing, anxious feeling in my stomach that I chalk up to hunger. It's lunchtime after all, and I haven't eaten since last night.

Eight hours after sunrise.

I lean against the pile of rocks. They dig into my back. Maybe Izzy's hurt, maybe she's lost, maybe she ran into trouble, because she's a magnet for trouble, maybe she's somewhere right now wishing she could reach me, but she can't.

Ten hours.

I'm pacing again.

Twelve hours after sunrise.

I turn toward the west. The sun is almost down. The sky is streaked with reds and pinks. I stare at it, at the clouds and the golden sun dropping below the horizon. My shoulders fall and I drop my head.

She's not here.

She's not coming.

I rub my hand down my face and let out a long shuddering sigh.

She's not coming.

Long shadows fall over the clearing. The birds have stopped singing.

I stare out at the woods, wondering what to do.

I drop to my knees next to the pile of rocks and start moving them aside. I clear them one by one. They're cool and rough and make a thunking sound as I toss them to the ground. When I get to the dirt I scoop it up with my hands. It's a combination of decomposing pine needles, leaf matter, dirt and roots. It's cold and moist. After a minute of digging I uncover the bright red lid of the peanut butter jar. I pull it out of the ground and dust it off on my jeans. Then I wipe my hands off. They're still dirty, and my nails have brown dirt under them, but it's good enough.

I sit back and stare at the closed jar. The two letters are still there. Although, I don't know why I would expect anything different.

The light now has a weak grayish cast. I slowly open the lid and dump the letters onto my lap. The first one I pull up is mine.

*I love you.*

*Marry me.*

I stare at the words for a moment and then I set the letter to the ground.

I pick up Izzy's and I slowly unfold it. I take in her words. I've never seen her writing before. It reminds me of her. It's a free-form, looping, dizzy cursive that I have to hold close to bring into focus. It's so much like her that it makes my chest ache.

I use the last remaining light of the day to read her words.

·  ·  ·

*Nathaniel,*

*The day we met was the anniversary of the day my fiancé died.*

*I was in a bad place, and I couldn't see that I'd find my way out of it. Life didn't work anymore, it hurt too much and I didn't see that it would ever get better. I'd been running, digging myself into a deep dark hole, trying to escape all that pain. But no matter where I went my grief chased after me. It was vengeful and suffocating and angry and bitter and desperate. And always there. No matter how much I smiled, or laughed, it was always there, just under the surface.*

*I figured I'd never feel love again. Never be able to let go. Not of the past I loved, and not of the future I dreamed of. I couldn't let go.*

*That day, I hit bottom. I couldn't go on. I didn't want to live anymore. So I prayed for help. For a sign that it was okay to go on, to live, to let go.*

*When I first saw you, I knew you were my sign. God or fate or David put you in my path. I thought they were looking down on me and you'd been sent to help me let go. And then when I learned you needed help too, I figured there wasn't any doubt. We were fated to help each other. So, I started the process of letting go.*

*I'm sorry.*

*When I taught you romance, I was replaying all the moments I had with David. Saying goodbye to him. The rowboat in the moonlight was our first date. The laugh and the story of the apple orchard. The poetry. The way he touched my face. The chocolates he gave me and what he said. It was all me, replaying the past.*

*It worked at first. The past was unraveling and I was saying goodbye. But then, the more we did together, the more you made everything your own. Our own. And I wasn't saying goodbye anymore, I was saying hello.*

*I'm sorry.*

*Because the more I started to fall in love with you, the more it hurt. Because instead of being happy, the grief for David, the part of me that never wanted to lose him, became angrier, more vengeful, more bitter. Because if I moved on from the pain, what would I have left of him? If I let go, what would be there to remind me of him? If there wasn't pain, what would there be?*

*They say you let go to make room for something better. But letting go made my grief howl with rage, because how could there be anything better than what I'd already had? What I'd dreamed of?*

*I'm sorry.*

*I love you. I know this is true. I love you.*

*You weren't just a sign sent to help me let go. You are the man I was meant to love.*

*The day you met me, you saved my life. I know you didn't realize that you did, you didn't know that you saved me, but you did.*

*I hope you understand that I need these six months to truly let go. To go back to my life and stop running and start letting go. So that when I come back to you, I can be free. So I can allow you to love me, and I can let myself love you.*

*Even though I said that you might realize these few days were crazy and you don't love me after all, I'll never stop loving you. You gave me the light again, for the first time in a year I can see the sun, and it's beautiful. But I'm not used to it yet, and it hurts to look at it. I need time.*

*Six months is a long time. I hope it's long enough.*

*If I'm not here, then I'm still trying. I'm still trying to let go.*

*I'm sorry if I've hurt you. I never meant to.*

*I hope that at this very moment I'm sitting next to you, that the pine needles are poking us and I'm holding your hand, telling you that I love you. Kissing you hello.*

*I'm sorry if I'm not.*

THE WORDS ON THE PAGE HAVE LONG GONE BLURRY, AND THE light has left the woods. My throat is raw as I stare at Izzy's letter. It's too dark to read now. I carefully fold it, trying not to get any dirt from my hands on it, and slip it in my pocket.

My heart feels battered, and I wish that she were here so I could hold her and tell her it's going to be okay. Or, I'd just hold her hand, and tell her when I do, that that means we're together. That I love her just as she is, whether that's laughing and trouble-making, or grieving and full of raging desperation and sadness. That I'd take her any way she is and any how she feels. As long as I get to love her.

I passed the spired church steeple on the way here. I remember Izzy saying the last time she'd been in Romeo, she'd only been to the church. I thought she'd meant for her aborted wedding, but she must've meant David's funeral.

The knowledge sits heavy on me.

She kept saying sorry in her letter, but there's nothing she has to be sorry for. Maybe she used me to recreate her memories with David, but then again, it didn't feel like I was being used. It felt, like she said, like we were saying hello. Like we were falling in love.

I believe in fate, and I think Izzy's right. She was led to me, and if she had to say goodbye at the same time she was saying hello, that's okay. It's alright.

I wish I could tell her it's alright.

Instead, I pick up my letter from the ground and gently refold it. I drop it into the plastic peanut butter jar and slowly screw the lid back on. Maybe she'll come back and dig this up. If she does, I want her to know how I feel.

To know that I still love her.

**33**

———

Nathaniel

Six Months Later...

I'm back in Romeo.

It's autumn again. I make the trip up every once in a while. For some reason, I feel like one of these times I'm going to walk into the pine tree copse and Izzy will be here.

She never is, but it feels like she will be.

Not for the first time I wish I had her phone number or some way of contacting her. But I don't. Months ago, I spent weeks searching for her online. But out of all the Izzy Harrises on the internet, not one of them was her.

I settle down to the ground and lean back against the rocks. There's a cloud in the sky that looks like a giant, fluffy teddy bear. It reminds me of Gertrude and Raphael's newborn.

It seems like the whole world is moving on.

Except me. I'm lying on the ground in this pine tree copse, and the world is passing by. I wonder if Izzy would tell me to let go. To move on.

It's been a year.

It's probably time to let her go.

I squint up at the sun, peaking in the sky.

I should let go, but I'm not quite ready.

**34**

―――――

ANOTHER YEAR LATER...

AUTUMN IN NEW YORK IS THE BEST.

I'm heading to Grand Central. It's the perfect day. The leaves in the parks are golden yellow and orange and the air is crisp and spiced with vendors selling candied nuts and coffee. I step aside so a dog walker, pulling half a dozen dogs down the sidewalk can pass by.

Life is good.

I've moved on.

I haven't been to Romeo or the pine copse in more than six months. I don't think about the plans I had, and I no longer imagine that Izzy's there, waiting under the pine tree for me. Just like with Gertrude, I needed to learn to let go of expectations.

Which is what Izzy said, isn't it? Don't expect. That way, no one can disappoint you, only pleasantly surprise you.

So, I no longer expect to marry a funny, laughing, adventure-loving woman with blonde wavy hair and mischievous eyes. And I don't expect to marry a sad-eyed woman who has been touched by grief but found her way through it.

In fact, although I still love that mischievous, trouble-making Izzy, I've let go of her. So I can make room for something better.

I stride down 42nd Street. I need to hurry if I'm going to be on time.

A little less than a year ago I expanded my consultation business. I now have six employees and an office rental space near the East River. Business is great. I was just on a call with one of our top clients, but it ran long. Because of that, I'm running behind.

I pick up my pace, glancing right then left, before hurrying across the street. I can see the statue of Mercury on top of Grand Central in the distance. I need to hop on the four train to make it to the Upper East Side on time.

My phone vibrates in my pocket. I pull it out and answer. "Hey Mom."

"You remember you're meeting Erma today, right?"

I smile. My mom has been pushing for this meeting since before I met Izzy. Back when I was picking out the ring for Gertrude my mom was begging me to go up and visit Erma.

"I remember," I say. "I'm heading there now."

"I'm glad. Don't be late. She's been asking to have lunch with you for more than two years. That's long enough to wait, don't you think?"

I smile, and then tease, "I don't know. I could drag it out a little longer. Maybe wait until Christmas?"

"Oh stop," she says. But I can tell she's happy. I didn't know it then, but my mom was worried about me when I was working my life down the drain at Wisebrook and Bleakerman. She's much happier now that I'm happy.

I say goodbye and hurry down the steps toward the train. I'm ready to move on.

**35**

———

Nathaniel

I make it on time to my lunch date with Erma.

She's chosen a French restaurant on the Upper East Side that serves light lunches, salads, and extravagant desserts with impeccable service.

They require that men wear a coat and tie and woman wear an equally decorous outfit.

Erma is in a big russet-colored hat and a matching silk shawl with a watercolor painting of trees in autumn on it. The hat dwarfs her, but you have to admit one thing, Erma has style.

At eighty-plus years old, she knows how to dress to impress. The style matches her black hair, dark eyes and fine-boned features.

When the hostess brings me to the table, Erma stands. I

bend down so she can give me a hug and a peck on the cheek. I pull her chair out and she sits back down, perching on the edge of her seat.

"I love visiting the city," she says with a twinkle in her eyes. "You never run out of things to do."

I pull out my chair and sit down across from her. We're at a table for four, so there is plenty of room. I notice that Erma has already ordered a pot of tea.

"I've always wanted to eat here," she continues. "One of my friends told me they have the best desserts."

"I'm sure they do," I say politely.

"Tea?" she asks.

"Please."

She pours the delicate apricot-colored liquid into a tea cup on my right. Steam rises from it.

"I hope you don't mind, I invited someone to join us."

I quickly look up from the steaming tea to Erma. "Sorry?"

She smiles at me and the wrinkles on her face deepen. "It's that accountant I told you about."

"Accountant?" Erma never told me about an accountant. I shake my head. "I'm sorry. I don't need an accountant. I've already hired one for the business."

Erma reaches across the table and pats my hand. "I mean your soul mate."

What? I give Erma a good, long look to make sure that she's serious. Sometimes she likes to mess with people. Joke around. But she has an earnest, pleased expression on her face.

So, she hasn't heard.

"Erma, I appreciate it, but Gertrude got married two years ago. She has a kid now. I'm sorry to tell you this, but she's not my soul mate."

Erma's eyebrows twitch and she looks confused. She pulls her hand from mine. "Who's Gertrude?"

It's my turn to be confused. "My soul mate?"

Erma shakes her head no. "I told you. Your soul mate is an accountant. She fits you perfectly." Erma looks me over. "Well, she fit the old you perfectly. She's elegant, polite, demure. She works hard at her job, she wants a family, and a home."

I imagine this person. This soul mate who sounds like the opposite of Izzy.

Well, I suppose I had to say goodbye to make room for the new.

"You'll meet her, won't you?" asks Erma.

I smooth the white tablecloth and look down at my reflection in the polished surface of the flatware. The diners at the other tables chat happily, there's soft classical music playing over the speakers, elegant flowers decorate the tables. It's the perfect environment to meet your soul mate. I look down at myself. I'm in a suit. The first I've worn in a long while. But I'm more relaxed, happier than I ever was wearing one before. And having finally, truly said goodbye to all expectations, to all plans, I am ready.

"I'll meet her," I say.

"That's wonderful," Erma says. "I wanted you to meet her years ago. But you've been hard to get ahold of and she hasn't been available either. She's been working at an international accounting firm in London for the past year and a half."

Erma keeps telling me more about how she found my soul mate, but I've stopped listening. There's a woman at the entry of the restaurant.

She hands her coat to the hostess and nods her thanks. My heart thunders in my ears. She's wearing a gray pencil skirt, a rose-colored cardigan with pearl buttons, and high heels. She's everything Erma said. Elegant. Polite. When she smiles at the hostess, I add demure.

She follows the hostess across the restaurant and I can't take my eyes away from her.

If there was such a thing as love at first sight, this is how it would feel.

I push my chair up and stand, never taking my eyes from her. She notices me for the first time, and when she does, a small smile flickers across her face.

Her smile hits me right in the chest.

*My word.*

She's my soul mate.

*Of course* she's my soul mate.

I step forward. She's still watching me, and there's a growing happiness in her expression that's echoed in my chest.

She feels it too.

I've never seen anyone smile like she's smiling right now. The sunlight from the window lands on her and she looks beautiful. More beautiful than any woman I've ever known.

Erma's voice fades back in. "...I met her years ago, when she was engaged to my godson...ah, here she is." Erma turns and stands. "So wonderful to see you, dear."

"Thank you. It's wonderful to see you," she says, and the honeyed sweetness of her voice nearly knocks me over.

I want to reach out and grab her, touch her, kiss her, make love to her, but all I can do is stand and stare. She turns to me and gives me a blinding smile.

"You're an accountant?" I ask, dumbstruck.

She nods, then says, "Hard to believe, isn't it? I've worked as an accountant for nearly ten years." She looks at me carefully, then says, "Except for that year I took off. I wasn't an accountant then."

I shake my head. "You're incredible."

Erma lowers her brow and looks between the two of us. "I'm sorry. Have the two of you already met?"

The woman lifts a delicately arched eyebrow, and the edges of her eyes crinkle in humor.

My chest expands at her look. Izzy was right. When you let go, you clear your heart out so all the good things in the world can come in.

"I'd be delighted if you introduced us," I say.

The woman gives me a mischievous look and then says to Erma, "My gran will be so happy to hear I've finally found my soul mate. She's been waiting for a baby for years and she wants me to get started right away." She looks down at her watch then back up at me. "I think probably, we could get started tonight."

Erma gives me a quick glance to see how I'm taking this odd pronouncement.

I'm taking it really, really well.

I rock back on my heels and grin at the woman.

"Oh. Goodness. Well then." Erma looks between us with

wide, owl-like eyes. I think my soul mate has managed to flap the unflappable Miss Erma.

She's got talent.

But Miss Erma rallies. "Darling, this is Nathaniel Barry. He's the grandson of my dear friend, and a wonderful businessman. He prefers to be called Nate—"

"Or Devon," I interrupt. "You can also call me Devon."

Erma scowls at me. "What in the world? That's not true. Don't call him Devon." Erma shoots me another scowl.

But I barely notice, I'm too busy taking in Izzy's grin.

"What if I call you 'love'?" she asks.

I think about it and then give a slow nod. "You could do that. Love would be alright."

Erma frowns. "This is the oddest introduction I've ever seen."

I grin at her. She didn't see our first introduction.

Erma continues. "Nate, this is Isabella Harris, the woman I've been telling you about."

"I prefer Izzy," she says. She reaches out and rests her hand on my arm. I feel a jolt at her touch. I reach up, take her hand, and thread it with my own.

"Izzy," I say.

"Or 'love,'" she says.

I nod. "Or 'love.'"

We stand, holding each other's hand, looking into each other's eyes. Erma is dumbstruck. She shakes her head and then plops down in her seat.

I touch Izzy's cheeks and her lips. Her eyes fill with tears and she squeezes my hand. Then she reaches into her purse and pulls out a folded piece of paper. It's torn, dirty, and wrinkled, but when she unfolds it I recognize the writing as my own.

She came back.

She came back to the pine copse.

I wasn't wrong to believe.

I swallow down the thickness in my throat.

The smile she gives me is full of so much joy, that I can't help myself, I lean down, cup her face with my hands, and kiss her. I kiss her and kiss her and kiss her. The room spins around us and I feel like I'm flying, but this time Izzy's with me.

She puts her hands on my shoulders and kisses me back.

When we pull apart, the waiter is at our table. Erma is politely ignoring us and placing an order for soup and salad.

"Did you two want anything to eat?" she asks. "I always find that kissing makes me hungry. Even if I'm not the one doing it."

Izzy puts a hand to her mouth and holds back a laugh.

"I'm sorry, Erma," I say, "but maybe, we can join you another time? I really want to...get to know Izzy."

"Hmmm," says Erma skeptically. She's nobody's fool. It's clear to every single person in this restaurant what Izzy and I are about to do. Then Erma shrugs. "Go on then. Tell your mother I said hello."

"Thank you," I say to Erma. And I mean it, more than she can know.

I grab Izzy's hand and start to pull her toward the door, but she tugs against me.

"Now hang on, Nathaniel. Are you really leaving without ordering some of these pastries? Didn't you see that pile of chocolate croissants? And chocolate mousse. And that's a tower of crème puffs. Do you see that?"

A happy feeling is growing inside me. It's so big that I can barely keep it contained.

I turn to the waiter. "Can I get a dozen chocolate croissants, two dozen crème puffs and a couple servings of chocolate mousse to go?"

The waiter scratches his chin and there's a gleam in his eye when he says, "Yes, sir."

I turn to Izzy. "How's that?"

She smiles at me. "You sure do know the way to a woman's heart, Nathaniel Barry."

I nod, "Mhm. I'm really glad we were introduced."

"Me too. Me too," she says.

She stands on her tiptoes, puts her hands on my shoulders and kisses me on the lips.

So I do the only thing a reasonably logical man would do with the love of his life. I grab her hand, the bag of full of pastries, and hurry out onto the beautiful autumn streets of New York.

"Care to take the train home?" I ask her.

She squeezes my hand. "Nathaniel, I'd take the train with you anywhere."

That sounds good to me. Better than good. It sounds like a lifetime of adventure.

# EPILOGUE

Izzy

THE SUBWAY ROCKS GENTLY.

I reach over and take Nate's hand. When I do, I feel like I'm holding all the happiness in the world.

It took two years, but I'm here. And it all started when I thought there was no reason to go on anymore—and then fate gave me Nathaniel.

But while I was trying to let go I realized I couldn't move forward if I was still hanging on to the past. And I really wanted to move forward—to this.

Nate looks down at our linked hands and smiles.

I scoot closer to him on the plastic subway bench seat.

"Where are we going again?" I ask.

"Home," he says.

I rest my head on his chest. "Where's that?"

He wraps his arm around me, pulls me close, then says, "Wherever you want it to be."

I settle against him. It feels like we were just sitting like this yesterday.

The subway glides through a tunnel and the lights flicker around us. We're moving forward. Together this time.

I think of something. "Did you ever go to Cinque Terre?"

Nathaniel's eyes crinkle at the corners. "Not yet."

Hmmm. I picture the Italian countryside, the towering cliffs, the sea, and the quaint towns, bakeries, coffee...and Nathaniel.

"What're you doing tomorrow?" I ask.

His grins and his eyes go all dark, showing me exactly what he'll be doing.

Ooookay.

"Or next week?" I amend.

He smiles approvingly.

Then he says, "Next week, I think I'll be having an adventure. In Italy. With my wife."

Oh, yes. I love him. I love him so much.

I stare at his happy expression, the line of his jaw, the turned-up corners of his lips.

"Izzy?"

"Hmmm?"

He grins. "This is where you say yes."

I laugh at the happiness bubbling inside me. He gives me that smile, the one that looks like the noonday sun, but this time it doesn't hurt, it feels a whole lot like love.

The subway slows and then the doors slide open. Nate

stands and holds out his hand. This is his stop. The way home.

I smile up at him, and I put the sun in my smile too. "Yes. Absolutely yes."

Nate grabs my hand and pulls me from the train in a joyous whirl.

It seems to me that when you ask the universe for a sign, it sure does know how to answer. It may take longer than you want, but eventually you'll get to your destination.

And then, another adventure can begin.

The train starts to pull away but Nathaniel and I are already running up the steps, to happiness, to our future, to adventure and to love.


THE END

# GET A BONUS EPILOGUE

Want more Izzy and Nate? Get an exclusive bonus epilogue for newsletter subscribers only.

When you join the Sarah Ready Newsletter you get access to sneak peaks, insider updates, exclusive bonus scenes and more.

Join Today!

www.sarahready.com/newsletter

# ABOUT THE AUTHOR

Author Sarah Ready writes contemporary romance and romantic comedy. Her books have been described as "euphoric", "heartwarming" and "laugh out loud". Her debut novel *The Fall in Love Checklist* was hailed as "the unicorn read of 2020".

Sarah writes stand-alone romcoms and romcoms in the Soulmates in Romeo series, all of which can be found at her website: www.sarahready.com.

Stay up to date, get exclusive epilogues and bonus content. Join Sarah's newsletter at www.sarahready.com/newsletter.

# ALSO BY SARAH READY

**Stand Alone Romances:**

The Fall in Love Checklist

Hero Ever After

Josh and Gemma Make a Baby

**Soul Mates in Romeo Romance Series:**

Chasing Romeo

Love Not at First Sight

Romance by the Book

Love, Artifacts, and You

Married by Sunday

**Stand Alone Novella:**

Love Letters

Find these books and more by Sarah Ready at:

www.sarahready.com/romance-books

Sign up to receive bonus content, exclusive epilogues and more at:
www.sarahready.com/newsletter